MEL TORREFRANCA

AVARIUM

A BELLADONNA NOVELLA

Lost Island
PRESS

MEL TORREFRANCA

AVARIUM

A BELLADONNA NOVELLA

Lost Island
—— P R E S S ——

Library of Congress Control Number: 2026906034

ISBN 978-1-962876-14-8 (paperback)
ISBN 978-1-962876-15-5 (ebook)

Cover illustration by Natalia Orshulevich
Select interior illustrations by Gonzalo Mansilla

Lost Island Press LLC
Oro Valley, AZ
lostislandpress.com

GUARDIAN DIVISIONS

RESEARCH

DEFENSE

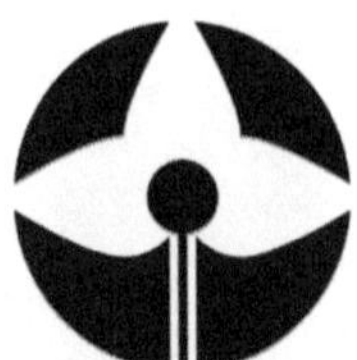

MEDICAL

For Sebastian

PART 1

INSTINCT

CHAPTER 1

WATCHDOG

Day 1 | 20 trainees remaining

♫ CLOSER TO THE MOON - ANYA NAMI ♫

Cal Avarium eats alone. Our first meal in the program made that clear.

When our instructors released all twenty of us into the dining hall for supper, my pulse raced at the sight of ten round tables, each seating only four. Belladonna Guardian Academy wanted us divided from the start.

Before I could blink, the other fifteen- and sixteen-year-olds started grabbing steel trays and forming little groups of twos, threes, and fours. They gawked at the chandeliers with hundreds of candles, the utensils made of genuine silver, and the way their voices echoed through the vast room.

"Too fancy!" one boy exclaimed. Maybe they felt that way about me too.

I grabbed a cold tray from the serving table and glanced at Avarium. No one had invited her either. She lingered back, tall and lean, her gray eyes hopping from boy to boy.

As soon as I took a step toward her, she darted for the last unclaimed table. Apparently, she hadn't been searching for someone to join; she'd been waiting to identify the spot where trainees would most likely leave her alone.

Well, fine by me. Avarium wasn't a good option anyway. To sit together would solidify our standing as *the girls*, and the eighteen boys in our cycle would dismiss us completely.

I scanned the room for an opening, and one boy sitting alone caught my attention. His hair was choppy—freshly cut, perhaps even yesterday. Clearly, he'd expected his selection for the program and intended to look good on his first day. And he did, though that didn't deter another boy from creeping behind him and flicking the back of his neck.

His head flinched forward, and a dollop of mashed potatoes fell off his spoon.

"Hey, pretty boy," said the trainee I called *Neck Flicker*.

The choppy-haired trainee straightened up and held his gaze. "You think I'm pretty?"

Neck Flicker's smile faltered.

"My name is Daxel Guppy," he continued, voice steady.

"Guppy?" Neck Flicker's smile snapped back into place. "Like the fish?"

Two boys at a nearby table did an awful job of stifling their laughter.

I gripped my tray tighter.

Danger.

Neck Flicker walked off while he had the upper hand, and I tracked him as he joined the two boys who'd been watching. The tall one had round glasses that shimmered in the chandelier light. The short one had more muscle than anyone else in the room. They looked like two goons pulled out of a children's book illustration.

I almost walked toward them until I recalled how they'd arrived at the Academy together—they were likely from the same school. To take their last empty chair would be bold. *Too* bold.

Danger.

My heart raced as I surveyed the other tables. I was running out of time.

On the opposite end of the room, by a wall made entirely of glass, two boys sat opposite each other. They smiled as they talked, but I sensed distance in their interactions—pauses between exchanges that lasted longer than those of friends.

Safe.

I nodded to myself and marched toward them.

"Hi!" I called, ensuring Neck Flicker and his friends would hear me and turn my way. *Invisible people don't get what they want.* That's what Mother always said, at least.

The two boys I approached raised their brows as if to ask, *Do we know you?*

I set my tray down, claiming a chair between them. It'd be stupid to request permission.

"I'm starving." I grabbed my utensils and started cutting into my steak. "You'd think the guardians would've had lunch prepared, considering how long the opening ceremony was. I haven't eaten since this morning, and *look*"—I gestured to the glass wall with my knife—"the sun's already setting."

The trainee to my left watched the sunset glaze the field and surrounding woods in an orange-pink hue. After a moment, he gave me an awkward smile. By the way he fidgeted with his fork, I couldn't tell if he was gathering the courage to shoo me off—or ask me on a date.

I swallowed my bite of steak. "Are you okay?"

He nodded, just barely.

"A girl, *and* she's from the City," said the boy to my right. He rested his chin on his fist and smiled, revealing his crooked buck teeth. "Quite the regrettable combination."

"Why do you say that, Big Tooth?"

He grinned even wider at the nickname. "Oh, you know why, Princess."

I *did* know why. Trainees from our capital rarely made the final five. People called us too entitled, too delicate. And being one of two girls selected this cycle didn't help my case either.

"What's your name?" he asked.

"Evaris."

"Evaris *what*?"

I hesitated. "Starfall."

"Starfall!" Big Tooth exclaimed. "You're from that family of fashion designers."

"I prefer my first name."

"You know, you can change your family name if you get married. Becoming a guardian won't do that for you. No need to fight through the program with us commoners."

I stabbed my fork into his fruit bowl and stole a grape.

Big Tooth squinted at me, shaking his head as I chewed. "What..."

To my left, the nervous one was tracing his steak knife along the tablecloth in some kind of pattern. He scowled at Big Tooth. "Oh, come on..."

While his intentions were in the right place, treating me as too delicate to handle a little taunting was offensive in its own right.

"Relax. He's right to assume I don't belong here. Even my family hates that I made the cut." I forced a smile. "So please, it's Evaris, not Starfall."

He smiled back, just barely.

"And you are?" I offered my palm.

It took him a second to unwrap his fingers from the knife he'd been playing with.

"I'm what?" he asked, his clammy hand meeting mine.

"Your name," I clarified, shaking his limp hand. Perhaps he thought I just wanted to hold it, which made me laugh.

"It's Boa."

"Hi, Boa." I let go, and he lowered his head, cringing.

I discreetly wiped my hand against my vest. Big Tooth chuckled at the sight.

"I'm Silver. Went to school with that guy, though I'm a grade older." He pointed at Daxel Guppy, the only other trainee sitting alone like Avarium.

"He doesn't seem like selection material," I muttered.

"You and him both, Princess." He stole a grape from *my* bowl this time.

I dug a spoon into my mashed potatoes, biting back a smile.

"Well, you're not a grade older than him anymore," Boa corrected. "We're all classmates now."

His comment made me pause mid-bite. Memories from the past few years flashed through my mind. Late nights studying by candlelight. Morning runs in the cold, the heat, rain or shine. Lectures from my parents, through shouts and tears alike. Shoves from classmates who wanted to prove I wasn't the fighting type.

The Academy instructors had selected us from across the Vakoi Empire, never more than three students from any one town. I was the best our capital had to offer, and I'd strutted in wearing the fanciest uniform.

But now we wore the same white button-ups, dark vests, blue ties, and annoyingly heavy boots. There were no grades anymore. No report cards. No class ranks. Being the best was just the entry fee.

Only five of us would graduate. The rest would go home.

And I can't go home.

I imagined my parents waiting for me on the steps to our grand estate. *Is it out of your system now? Are you finally ready to take your life seriously?*

I imagined walking back into Vakoi City Secondary, my classmates grinning as I took my old seat. *You're not strong after all.*

Silver's voice reeled me out of my spiral. "Did you talk to your roommate yet, Evaris?"

Boa dropped his fork, his eyes widening as it clattered against his tray.

I tilted my head, but he said nothing. Only picked up his fork and kept eating.

"Uh... briefly," I answered.

"What'd you talk about?" Silver asked, oddly curious.

"Nothing." Well, nothing of substance. I had asked Avarium exactly one question earlier, as we changed into our new uniforms: Where are you from? She had replied with a single word—Sitra—and hadn't bothered to ask me anything in return.

"Don't be coy." Silver set his utensils down, hungry for gossip instead of steak. "You must have talked about *that*."

"Huh?"

"You know, *that*."

I blinked. Either I'd missed something, or he was making a weird joke.

"Oh," Boa said. "You haven't heard."

Silver leaned toward me. "You really haven't?"

I gestured between them. "Just tell me already."

Silver smiled deviously with those big buck teeth of his. "Your roommate is a murderer."

"No she isn't." It came out like a reflex.

"Is too. She killed a boy in the woods. And the guardians only locked her up for four months before sending her here with the rest of us."

"Didn't you read the article?" Boa asked.

I shook my head. I rarely read *Capital Weekly*. If the news were important, it'd find its way to me, I always told myself.

"That doesn't make sense," I said. "The guardians wouldn't select a criminal."

"Apparently, they already had their eyes on her before it happened," Boa explained.

"And honestly, why waste her?" Silver shrugged. "She had the highest scores in her class, and I heard she can run a five-minute mile."

It was borderline believable. I couldn't break seven minutes myself.

Boa shuddered. "I heard someone tried to drown her, and she crawled out of the lake twenty minutes later."

My throat tightened. I looked over at my roommate's table, where she chewed on a bite of steak, knife in hand. Her porcelain skin and silky black hair were almost doll-like.

I faced the boys again. "Do you know how she killed him?"

"The article didn't mention that," Silver said. "For a reason, I assume."

Boa cleared his throat. "But everyone's saying that—"

Silver clapped his hands over his ears. "I don't want to hear it again."

Boa leaned in to whisper, "Log."

I frowned. "Huh?"

"She struck him over and over, on the head, with a *log*."

I scaled the spiral staircase alone that night, with nothing but the Academy's wall-mounted torches to guide me. I had spent the last couple of hours socializing with Boa, Silver, and a handful of other boys in the common room on the first floor. I downplayed my posh background and smiled at the right times—it was almost too easy to get along. There was plenty of laughter among us while the sky darkened.

I stepped off the landing onto the second-floor lobby. It was cozy and cluttered, unlike most of the rooms in this monster of a building. Sofas. Chessboards. Bookshelves with novels. There were darts propped up in tin cans, but not the kind used for combat—these were playful with feathered tips, and some already pierced the dozens of cork targets on the walls.

Ten numbered doors lined the walls of the lobby, each leading to a trainee living quarter. There were two of us per room, but at some point, there would be one each, and even later, there would be five vacant and five occupied by the winners. The filtrations would decide, with time, which of us deserved to stay.

I stopped at the door to Room 4.

"...killed a boy in the woods..."

"...struck him over and over..."

I gripped the doorknob firmly, and with a quick twist, stepped inside.

A warm, howling breeze brushed my cheeks.

The only sign of Avarium was the balcony door, which she had left ajar. The curtains breathed with the nightly wind.

I struck a match and lit the handheld lantern on my nightstand.

I scanned our narrow balcony. Empty.

I checked our private restroom. Empty.

Weird.

I stood in the space between our beds, lantern in hand, spinning in a slow circle as though Avarium might materialize behind me.

"...killed a boy..."

"...struck him..."

I stopped and took a deep breath. I hadn't read the article myself—perhaps Boa and Silver were exaggerating. Maybe Avarium had her reasons.

I grabbed the pajamas from my bed and headed to the restroom for my first shower at the Academy. There were more lanterns in my room back home, so it was eerie to wash off without much light. This would be an adjustment for sure. I'd never shared a living space with a stranger before, and certainly not a room this small. I didn't even have my book collection and my favorite quilts to comfort me.

But at least the soap was peppermint and smelled nice.

I dried off. My golden pajamas were smooth and draped like a second skin. Normally, silk repulsed me, but I appreciated the simple elegance of this piece—monochromatic with matching buttons, not noisy like typical Starfall attire. It was the first luxury that didn't remind me of my family.

A few years back, when I was thirteen, I had spent every gifted coin on casual, dark clothes my parents wouldn't approve of, just to spite them. In the face of their rage, something clicked. If I could defy them in something small, I could defy them in something bigger.

This was it—guardianship.

Finally, a path of my own.

I stepped out of the restroom and froze in my tracks.

Avarium was sitting on her bed, staring as though she'd been waiting. Her long, black hair—parted straight down the middle—draped over her shoulders symmetrically. It took her several seconds to blink.

I broke eye contact and started re-arranging the pillows on my bed.

"I didn't see you earlier," I said, grabbing the only novel I'd brought from home.

"What book is that?" Her voice was deeper than I'd expected.

I moved my fingers so she could read the title.

Avarium leaned and squinted, but had nothing to say.

I got into bed, novel in hand. It took all I had to resist the urge to look over the pages. I couldn't tell if she was still sitting there, watching me.

She was a murderer. She had killed a boy, had struck him over and over, with a *log*.

According to Boa and Silver, at least. They hadn't sounded like they were making it up, but perhaps it was an elaborate joke to rattle me. If only someone else had spoken during recreation time to confirm the rumor. I knew better than to ask and risk looking like either a coward or a fool.

Had Avarium really slept in a cell last night—the same night before sharing a room with me?

She shuffled into bed. "Goodnight, Evaris."

I frowned at the pages. I hadn't told her my name.

"Goodnight, Avarium," I replied.

She hadn't told me hers either.

CHAPTER 2

SCAPEGOAT

Day 8 | 20 trainees remaining

♫ SNOWFLAKES - FORGOTTEN GARDEN ♫

Cal Avarium was always on time. In fact, she was often the first to arrive. During our initial week in the program, she acted as though the bell was a death toll for anyone late, and I had no idea why. All I knew was that she had *focus*. Real, unwavering focus that I'd never witnessed before in my life. She absorbed Professor Embre's lectures without fidgeting with her pencil, tapping her foot, or mouthing words while jotting them down. She simply blinked, read, wrote...

I, on the other hand, could barely hold my attention for ten minutes at a time. My desk partner, Boa, occasionally tapped his pencil against my notebook, urging me to stay focused. Most of my effort went into holding back yawns so Professor Embre wouldn't snap again. She was in her mid-twenties, I presumed, not far removed from her own time in the program, and it showed in the way she treated us like rivals. To her, we were foolish, sloppy mistakes—not winning material like her. She never missed a chance to remind us.

That morning was no exception. I was nodding off when Professor Embre stopped talking mid-sentence.

Whispers of trainees replaced the scribbling of their pencils.

I straightened and blinked myself awake.

The boy we called *Gup* stood in the doorway, twenty minutes past the bell.

"Daxel!" Professor Embre shouted. "For the glory of Vakoi, *what* are you wearing?"

He smoothed his hands over the front of his golden shirt. "My pajamas, Professor."

She leaned back as though he'd struck her.

A few boys turned their heads, shielding grins from Professor Embre. The rest of us shot daggers at Toll, Gup's roommate. We had all seen the neck flicks, the shoulder shoves, the snides and snickers... He was using Gup to send a message that he belonged on top, among the winners—and unfortunately, he had the background to support it. Toll and his two goons had come from Miranda Secondary, the school with the highest Academy selection *and* graduation rate in the Vakoi Empire.

"This is funny?" Professor Embre's head swerved, and anyone who *was* smiling forgot why. "You think the Force looks favorably upon jokes like this?"

Gup took a step toward her and raised his voice. "It's not a joke, Professor."

"Then explain to me why you're dressed for bed."

He hesitated, eyes darting to his roommate.

Toll stared back with a stern expression. He seemed strangely unamused by his own prank.

Gup lowered his head. "I don't know."

I frowned, thinking back to our first supper at the Academy. Gup had responded to Toll's *pretty boy* insult with, *"You think I'm pretty?"* And he'd done just as well at handling him this past week, never showing a flicker of embarrassment, and occasionally even spouting a clever insult of his own. Had Toll finally pushed him too far, or was I missing something? Why didn't Gup take the opportunity to snitch?

Professor Embre pointed to the hallway. "You're dismissed."

"Is there any chance I could get a new set of uni—"

"*Now*," she snapped.

Gup's eyes widened, but he knew better than to argue.

As soon as he stepped outside the lecture hall, Professor Embre slammed the door behind him. The sound shook the floors, and her sweeping glare sent goosebumps up my arms.

She snatched a piece of chalk and resumed her lecture.

The tall Miranda boy with the glasses smiled and discreetly nudged Toll's arm.

Toll brushed him off, lips pursed, eyes glued to the blackboard.

Something isn't adding up.

I did my best to pay attention to the lecture, but every so often, I snuck a glance at Toll. He kept biting his nails and scanning the room.

Turns out, Avarium was watching him too. It was the first time I saw her break focus during class.

They served beet juice in the dining hall that day. They always did.

Silver raised his glass for a toast. "To the best cranberry farms in the Vakoi Empire."

"You wish," I said, yet I still watched with anticipation as he took a sip. Secretly, I was wishing for the same thing. *Cranberry juice would be nice for a change.*

Silver's lips formed an open-mouthed pucker, his buck teeth on full display. I almost expected him to growl.

"Great, beets again," I inferred.

Boa took a big gulp. "You two had better drink up. When the guardians start adding poison, we'll need to down this stuff every day."

Silver rolled his eyes. "They're not gonna poison us, Boa."

I yawned and pushed my glass aside.

"Listen." Boa leaned in. "Every guardian memoir I've read has mentioned poison in the Academy beet juice. Maybe they haven't laced our drinks yet, but one of these days, they *will*, and it'll keep happening."

Boa loved clinging to illusions of control. He told me he'd been making his bed every morning in case the guardians filtered trainees who didn't. It was a baseless assumption, but it made him feel better, so I didn't challenge him.

Silver, on the other hand, had discovered his favorite hobby was challenging Boa.

"Assuming you're right," he said, "how will drinking this help me?"

"You'll get used to the flavor."

"Okay, and?" Silver laughed. "How will that make me less sick later?"

Boa's face paled as he lowered his glass.

Checkmate.

Silver smirked. Sometimes I wondered if he only sat with Boa and me because it made him feel big. He'd been spending recreation time with Toll and the other two Miranda boys over the past few days, yet he still didn't claim the fourth open seat at their table in the dining hall. He even passed Boa memoirs he thought he'd like and helped me train at night. Maybe he enjoyed playing both sides—feeling pushed by one group and being the *pusher* for the other.

"So, what do you think, Evaris?" Silver stuffed his mouth with chicken and rice.

"About Boa's poison theory?"

"About Gup," he answered, still chewing. "What do you think he did to piss Toll off?"

"Don't talk with your mouth open."

"Sorry, Princess."

I nearly took a bite of chicken but stopped myself to consider his question. It was a curious question indeed. I had never considered that Gup might have instigated Toll's treatment of him, yet Silver had assumed such from the start.

"What makes you think he's acting in vengeance?" I finally took my next bite.

"I've talked to the guy quite a bit these past few days. He doesn't seem like the type to be a nuisance for no reason. Gup gave him a motive. The question is *what*?"

I narrowed my eyes. "Way to blame the victim."

"I said what I said."

"Hey, look," Boa interrupted, staring off at my roommate's table. "Avarium's not here."

We all called her that. Avarium. It wasn't a group decision; it just sort of happened. The name Cal could belong to a neighbor or a friend. Avarium was cold and clinical. Far more fitting, considering she was the Force's experiment, the murderer they took a chance on.

Alleged murderer, at least. I still hadn't seen the article Boa and Silver had told me about—our instructors didn't allow us contact with the outside world. But the story had spread among trainees, and some even claimed to have read the article themselves. Most likely, she had really killed someone. I just didn't know why.

I looked at her usual table. Vacant. She had always arrived on time for breakfast, lunch, supper—and classes, of course. She even showered within the same ten-minute window every night.

"Gup isn't here either." Silver's lips spread into a smile with lots of teeth. "He must be her next victim."

I scowled, hoping it'd keep him from running his mouth. It did not.

"Just hear me out, okay? Toll was acting strange this morning. Don't tell me you didn't see it too. I don't think he smiled *once* during Research class. Maybe *Avarium* was the one to mess with Gup's uniforms."

Boa's eyes widened. "She could sabotage Gup's attendance while also hurting Toll's reputation—he's an easy scapegoat."

I studied Avarium's table, and the scene played in my head without permission: my roommate, in the middle of the night, sneaking into Toll and Gup's room. Opening Gup's dresser without a sound. Gathering his uniforms. Burning them. Cutting them. Or otherwise destroying them. Then crawling back into bed across from me, as though she'd done nothing.

I rubbed my forehead. It was aching again.

"Maybe she's landing a finishing blow, right as we speak." Silver gestured around. "See any logs?"

The dining hall door burst open, and we looked over in unison.

Avarium stood in the doorway, ten minutes late.

And beside her was Gup, still in his pajamas.

"Next victim," Silver whispered. "I'm calling it."

The latecomers brought their trays to Avarium's usual table and chatted as though no one was staring. Something Avarium said made Gup smile. He didn't seem to care that she had murdered a boy back home, and she didn't seem to care that he was wearing his pajamas.

"It was Toll," I said. "Not her."

"Or that's what she wants us to believe," Silver said in a creepy campfire-like tone.

I frowned at Toll, who received glares from all directions.

"It wasn't me," he said, to no one in particular.

I didn't blame Gup for skipping our afternoon classes—Defense, especially. Our training instructor, Commander Roz, was a middle-aged guardian with a neatly trimmed beard and narrow eyes. On average, he was less strict than Professor Embre, but he could snap sometimes. To me, this unpredictability made him more terrifying than her consistent rigidity. If Gup were to show up in his pajamas, there was a good chance he would've kicked him out too.

Plus, Defense class itself was awful. For our first week, we'd been running hand-to-hand combat drills for the entire two-hour block, hardly taking breaks—and even then, only for water. Commander Roz said we couldn't start training with blades until we sharpened our most essential tool first —our bodies. The whole process of *sharpening* was a pain in the ass. I vomited once and had to clean up the mess.

A couple of times, I had contemplated skipping Defense class myself. Perfect attendance wasn't required, though being absent was a gamble. If a filtration took place, you'd lose by default and get sent home. It was a risk I would have warmed up to, if not for a bigger consequence attached— appearing weak-willed in front of the others. So I showed up every single day.

If only someone could sabotage *my* uniforms so I could take time off without shame. I was sleep-deprived, sore, and mentally foggy. This was a soul-crushing routine that only a rare few thrived in, while the rest shrank a bit more each day. *Slip*, we called it—because anyone could hang on, but not everyone could hang on for long. Boa claimed to have read about trainees filtering themselves or purposefully botching filtrations to get sent home.

I wondered if I was the type to slip, or the kind to cling.

"Single file!" Commander Roz yelled.

We scattered into place in the dimly lit training room. There were no windows—just sleek walls of dark stone covered with mounted torches and guardian tools. It always felt like night, even in the early afternoon.

I fought back a yawn as Commander Roz walked our line, staring us down. He looked like the kind of man who had spent years tracing members of the Underground, and he probably had. The dual swords strapped to his back caught the torchlight, and I wondered who he'd killed with them. I wondered what their stories were.

"Today's our first sparring practice. Half power, half speed—we're learning, not conditioning. Use combinations from the drills we've been running." He stopped in front of me. "Evaris, you're with Cal."

"Yes, Commander."

What a surprise. He had paired me with Avarium for drills every day, so of course she'd be my sparring partner too. Perhaps he wanted to sabotage our success by never forcing us to face opponents beyond each other.

Our first sparring match proved me wrong—I was no equal to Avarium. Her strikes were almost too fast to keep up with, and I winced every time I blocked her with an arm bar, certain the impact would leave a bruise. I couldn't tell if she was ignoring Commander Roz's order to use half power, half speed, or if she was really *this* good.

Within a few minutes, she landed a blow to my chest that I failed to dodge. Commander Roz reprimanded *me* instead of her.

"Keep your head straight, Evaris. You're distracted."

"Sorry, Commander."

"Have you been sleeping?"

"Yes, Commander."

"Doesn't look like it." He handed me a chilly canister. "Drink up."

Avarium and I watched the boys spar during our water break. Some of them, like Silver and Nash, would throw too many punches and kicks, attempting to emulate rabid beasts. Others, like Boa and Krevall, would think too hard, get in their heads, and miss every chance to take a shot.

Avarium would wait, but never for too long. Even in combat, she was always on time.

Commander Roz circled the room, watching us, occasionally correcting us. But he always lingered by Avarium the longest—and he never had much to say. Once I noticed this, I couldn't unsee it. Perhaps, just one week in, he was already betting on her making the final five.

Perhaps she was capable of more than I believed.

GHOSTWALKER

Day 8 | 20 trainees remaining

♫ EASIER TO LAUGH - COURTNEY FARREN ♫

Cal Avarium could run a five-minute mile. I didn't believe it until I saw it myself.

Field class at the Academy ran on a rotating schedule, our three instructors taking turns throughout the week. It could be the best class of the day—or the worst. Professor Embre was teaching this time, making it the latter. She stood in the grassy field that surrounded the Academy building, her boot-length overcoat and dark curls swaying in the summer breeze. The bow and quiver of arrows strapped to her back shimmered in the late-afternoon light.

"One mile," Professor Embre said, "equals one lap along the treeline."

Avarium kept up with the boys. In fact, she passed most of them. Made top three.

I was last. Professor Embre made everyone wait for me. When I finally slowed to a stop, my calves cramped up, and every part of my body, all the way to my neck, went stiff. I hadn't been running this past week, especially with all the exercise Defense training put us through. Perhaps I'd already lost my stride.

"Are you sick, Evaris?"

I leaned over with my hands on my knees. "No, Professor." The words came out breathless.

"I was hoping you'd say yes."

One of Toll's goons chuckled. It was the short and stocky Miranda boy.

Professor Embre's eyes attacked him without missing a beat. "Am I funny to you, Nash?"

"No, Professor." Nash paused and swallowed his humor. "I-I mean, you're funny when you're trying to be. You *can* be funny."

Beside him, Krevall fought off a grin. He removed his glasses to distract himself and wiped them on a small, untucked piece of his button-up.

Strangely enough, Toll didn't make eye contact with Nash or Krevall. Out of the Miranda trio, he was usually the first to find humor in anything. But like this morning, after Gup had appeared in his pajamas, Toll stared at Professor Embre and waited for class to resume.

"Woods, everyone," she ordered. I could have sworn her lips curved upward a little.

Our group of nineteen trainees followed Professor Embre into the trees surrounding the field. Gup still wasn't here—no point in showing up just for her to throw him out again.

Boa and Silver appeared next to me, but they didn't mention my run time. They didn't say anything at all.

My cheeks warmed up. They felt sorry for me. That was it. What a fool I'd made of myself. I had expected to run slower than most of the boys— but Avarium, the only other girl, had risen to the top. I had no excuse for my pathetic performance.

It was easy to see which of us had the most dedication.

After trekking for a few minutes into the woods, Professor Embre demonstrated our field lesson for the day. She crept over various surfaces —rocks, twigs, beetles, dead leaves—without making a sound.

Now it was our turn. We split up in the general area, practicing solo in our own little stretches of ground. It was meticulous to an infuriating degree, and I would have thought it impossible, had I not seen Professor Embre walk like a ghost just a moment ago.

She made her rounds between us, offering suggestions and minor corrections. But for some reason, she lingered near me the most, and not in the way Commander Roz hovered by Avarium. She kept shouting, *Heel to toe, Evaris! Bend your knees!*

At one point, I stomped forward just to spite her.

She appeared out of nowhere and pushed me off my feet.

I scratched my palm on a twig as I tried to break my fall. It was a failed effort anyway—my chin landed on a rock, earning me a jagged cut.

The other trainees stopped their solo practices and looked my way.

I pushed myself to my knees and touched my chin. The sight of blood on my fingers made me cringe.

"Get up."

Boys whispered as I rose. I could feel Professor Embre's big eyes glaring at the back of my neck. She made my skin crawl.

"Stomping like that would get your entire unit killed."

I took a deep breath and pivoted to face her. "Sorry, Professor," I muttered, hoping she'd end the lecture there. Everyone was watching. *Again.*

"Members of the Force don't work alone. If one guardian is careless, others pay for their mistake. That's why we have five winners, not twenty. Only the most competent can be trusted. Are *you* competent?"

I frowned. "Yes, Professor."

"Wipe that blood off your chin and prove it."

I winced, rubbing a hand under my cut. The sight of my red palm made my stomach churn, so I quickly wiped it on my pants and got into position.

As my fellow trainees resumed their practice, Professor Embre raised her voice. "Did I tell the rest of you to keep going?"

Everyone stopped.

"Let's all watch Evaris try again."

Silver made eye contact, squinting as though I'd disappointed him. Boa eagerly nodded, urging me to follow Professor Embre's order quickly.

My legs shook as I walked. A twig snapped under my boot.

"Heel to toe!" Professor Embre shouted. "Bend your knees!"

I bent my knees and tried again. Another twig broke.

"Bend your knees!"

"They *are* bent!"

She shoved me down again, and this time, I stayed down.

"Everyone else, back to it." Professor Embre took a step forward, casting me in her shadow. "Evaris, need I dismiss you?"

I shuffled on the ground to face her. "No, Professor."

"Get up."

I complied and continued practicing, my hands rolled into fists. Every so often, I scanned my surroundings, paranoid Professor Embre would sneak up on me again—which unintentionally led me to catch several boys staring instead. In the program, my behavior earlier might as well have been a tantrum.

Finally, Professor Embre released us for recreation time. I didn't look at her as I rushed toward the Academy building.

She snatched my wrist from behind me. "Evaris."

My breath hitched. I looked over my shoulder.

A few boys were nearby, so she leaned toward me and whispered, "I vouched for you because of your strong will. Use that *for* the Force, not against it. I am not your enemy."

With that, she let go.

I rubbed my sore wrist. No one back in Vakoi City had supported my choice to train for the Academy. My blood still boiled from what Professor Embre had put me through, but something else—something almost like gratitude—crept in too. I hated not knowing what to feel.

Before I knew it, I was running. Across the field, into the building, up the staircase toward my room...

The two-hour block between field class and supper was always the most scattered time of day. Some trainees would shower off the sweat of our afternoon classes, while others would study in the library or exercise in the training room.

Silver would likely stay outside to run laps around the field with Toll, Krevall, and Nash for the fourth day in a row. I didn't understand how he put up with the Miranda boys, but I wasn't one to judge. I knew a girl who'd go around vandalizing murals in Vakoi City. Not my proudest moment, tagging along.

I'd normally sit with Boa in the dining hall during recreation time—hardly anyone was there outside of meals, so it was always calm. He'd let me review his Research notes, which helped loads, because mine were scarce. Meanwhile, he'd read guardian memoirs from the library, occasionally interrupting me with an interesting tidbit.

Not today, though. I needed to be alone for a while. My chin was bleeding, and my chest still ached from Avarium's *half-power* punch.

I rushed off the landing into the lobby and stopped at the sight of Gup in his gold pajamas. He sat on a sofa, reading a novel called *The Wishing Bridge* without sparing me a glance. But he made a rookie mistake—his eyes hardly moved, and his tight grip on the pages told me that he was on high alert. After what Toll had done to his uniforms, I didn't blame him for not wanting to be alone in his quarter, waiting for his roommate to return.

We're both having a terrible day, aren't we?

"Hey Gup." I waved.

His eyes widened at my bleeding chin.

I'd only spoken to him once before, during Defense class, when we'd bumped into each other and muttered a quick *sorry*. That was it. None of us wanted to associate with him and risk becoming the Miranda boys' next target. But with no one else around, I found myself wanting to help.

"Could I see your clothes, if you still have them?"

Gup stared a moment longer before leaving his novel behind. He entered his quarter and shut the door. Maybe he planned to ignore me.

I nearly left for my room, but he stepped out just in time with a bundle of torn fabric in his arms.

"They're not really clothes anymore," Gup said.

I plucked a few pieces and stretched them out. This was the work of scissors, which made them fixable. The saboteur hadn't been smart enough to burn them or dye them with chemicals.

I flinched when the Academy's front door opened on the floor below us. Trainees were catching up, and I couldn't have them see me with Gup.

I'd given everyone enough to gossip about already.

"Quickly," I said, rushing to the staircase.

Gup followed me up to the fifth floor.

The infirmary was down the hall from the Medical lab, where we spent our late-morning classes with Doctor Blimmery. It was even smaller than our trainee quarters and contained nothing but a few simple beds, a single window, and a wall of white cabinets. This was likely the same room where the uniform-cutter had found scissors. And now I, the uniform-fixer, was in the same place the crime had been committed to repair the damage.

I opened the closest cabinet and rummaged for stitching supplies. If there was any place on the grounds with needles, this would be it.

"You should look for a bandage while you're at it," Gup said.

I dodged his concern. "Can you put your clothes on one of the beds?" I'd clean the cut under my chin later so it wouldn't get infected, but not in front of him. It was going to sting like hell.

Gup laid his clothes out on one of the beds. "How'd it happen?"

"Uh... I fell during field class. It's nothing, really." He would surely hear the true story later, but at least I could save the embarrassment for now.

"Looks pretty bad."

I pushed a few unlabeled containers aside. It took a few more minutes to find a little white box labeled *STITCHING*. The suture thread it contained wouldn't match Gup's uniforms, but it'd be strong enough to hold everything together.

I cut a piece of thread and slipped it through the eye of the needle. "I could use your help with the puzzle. You know, getting the right sets back together. Can you find the ones that line up, and put them in piles?"

Gup nodded and worked on separating the fabric, each group representing a single set. As soon as he identified two pieces that belonged together, I got to work.

"You really think you can fix them?"

I grinned. "I'm doing it right now."

Gup arranged more pieces for me. "I guess I should trust you, considering you're a Starfall."

It was quiet, nothing to hear but the soft rustling of fabric. I could have done everything faster with the right equipment back home, but before I knew it, I had pieced together an entire set—shirt, tie, vest, and all.

Gup chuckled. "Almost looks new."

I tilted my head. "It's patchy."

For the first time, he smiled at me—just like he'd smiled at Avarium during lunch. I wondered what she'd said to him earlier. Maybe my curiosity was another reason why I'd offered to help.

"Thanks, Evaris."

"It's nothing, really."

"Thanks," he repeated, firmer. He wanted me to hear him.

"You're welcome." I moved on to another set. "Maybe as a reward, you could answer some questions."

"I'll give you three."

I took my time, considering where to start. Eventually, I asked, "Why didn't you snitch on Toll this morning?"

"Because I'm not certain he did this." Gup held up two pieces, considering how they might fit together. "I mean, he *could* have. But I doubt it. I've gone to school with guys like him. They're not bullies, just bugs. Plus, he was freaked out this morning. Kept telling me he was being framed."

Perhaps that explained Toll's odd behavior today. I replayed my observations of him in my head and nearly pricked my finger as a result. Unlike my family, I couldn't sew while distracted—it took intense focus to avoid finger bandages.

"Second question," I said. "Why'd you sit with Avarium at lunch?"

"Because she invited me."

"Why?"

"I don't know. And now you're out of questions."

"The *why* doesn't count. Come on, play fair."

"Fine. One more. But that's it."

"Okay, one more question..." A smile found its way to my lips. "I saw you reading *The Wishing Bridge* earlier. Such a classic."

I paused for dramatic effect. He raised a brow.

"Who's your favorite character so far?"

It was obvious, with the look on my face, that I had seen through his fake reading.

Gup laughed through a scoff. "Oh *shut it*!"

I started laughing too, which made him laugh harder. And before I knew it, I had pricked my finger on the needle, but I hardly felt a thing.

I didn't show up to supper. Frankly, I didn't want to face everyone after the atrocity of field class. I could start fresh tomorrow. Hopefully any gossip would die down after a night of rest.

Silver wouldn't let me off the hook so easily. He knocked on my door at 9:30 sharp, the exact time we normally met in the courtyard out front. The night bell tolled at 10:00, but it was more of a suggestion to sleep than an order. With rooms kept open, most trainees stayed up to study, exercise, or chat and decompress. Sometimes, Toll, Krevall, and Nash hosted dart-throwing competitions in the lobby, keeping the rest of us up with their cheering. We each hoped someone else would have the guts to scold the Miranda boys, and as a result, no one did.

I normally spent my nights with Silver, running through Commander Roz's drills. He had offered to help me play catch-up a few days ago, after I'd vomited in Defense class. We could train together outside, he'd said— it was cool enough at night, even in the summer, and we could avoid the boys who hogged the training room.

At first, I wondered what was in it for him. But I figured soon enough that Silver enjoyed being better than me and showing off a little. I really did need the help, so I put up with it.

Silver knocked on my door a second time. "Wake up, Princess!"

I rolled my eyes and greeted him, already dressed in my pajamas.

"Someone's running late."

I shrugged. "I'm just not training tonight."

His lips parted, buck teeth jutting forward. "Well, why not?"

"I'll get back on schedule eventually." I tried to close the door, but he stopped it gently, and I let him.

"You're slipping, Evaris." He eyed the bandage on my chin.

"I'm *not*."

"Are too. What was that scene all about? In field class."

"Oh, shut it."

"No. I know you're tired, but we're *all* tired. Stop being a City girl, and come practice with me."

"I said no, Silver."

He took a step forward. "But you need to—"

"Back up, Big Tooth!"

His eyes widened.

An instant pit formed in my stomach. Skipping supper certainly didn't help.

Without another word, Silver backed into the lobby.

I shut the door between us and leaned my forehead against it, unsure of what to do. Perhaps I needed to rush out and apologize. I hadn't heard him walk away, so he was still there, wasn't he?

I took a breath and opened the door as quickly as I'd closed it. "Sorry, I—"

But Silver was gone, like a ghost.

I proceeded to pace the length of my quarter. For the second time today, I'd thrown a tantrum. Perhaps I really *was* slipping. Maybe I didn't have the drive that everyone else did. While the others were here to pursue prestigious careers as guardians, I had *come* from prestige. I'd grown up within a ten-minute walk from Vakoi Palace. My sole purpose for being here was to prove to my family that I didn't need to be their version of a Starfall to be valuable. Was that enough?

With a sigh, I got into bed with a book. Stories were always a great tool for disappearing. Even in solitude, I could pretend I was safe, with people around who understood me, looked after me, and made me laugh. I had first noticed this at eight years old—it was far easier to relate to book characters than the neighbors' kids my parents pushed me to play with.

About an hour later, Avarium returned from wherever she went at night —I hadn't worked up the courage to ask. She stretched her arms on the other side of the room, and I looked over my pages, stealing a glimpse. She was more focused than I could ever be. We had only been here a week, and

I was already contemplating whether I had what it took to stay.

She met my gaze. "What book is that?"

I blinked. Avarium rarely initiated conversation with me.

"Hello?" she said.

I blurted the title aloud, to which she had no response. It felt unsettling to let the conversation die there.

"Do you want to read the description?" I offered.

Avarium sat on her bed and gazed through our balcony's glass door, up at the stars. She did that a lot. "Maybe once I get out of here."

I frowned. It was an honor to get *into* the Academy, yet she spoke as though the program were a roadblock. If she were anyone else, I'd pry for more information, but it seemed reckless to ask a murderer questions that she might not like, especially in a room alone with her.

I continued reading. A few minutes later, Avarium cleared her throat. "Hey."

She was staring at *me* now, not at the glass. I wondered how long ago she'd made the switch.

"Gup said you helped him with his uniform."

My pulse quickened. "Were you... with him tonight?"

She shrugged. "Around."

I didn't know what that meant—but frankly, I was less interested in their budding friendship and more concerned that word would get loose. If the boys asked Gup about his uniform, would he rat me out? *I should have told him to keep his lips sealed.*

"Don't tell anyone." It came out ruder than intended, so I added, "Please."

She nodded to herself as if she'd just solved a puzzle. "You're trying to avoid negative attention."

"Who isn't?" I said. "People can either help you, or get in your way."

The sky stole her gaze again. "So that's why you never sit with me."

I wondered if that was the real answer she'd been fishing for. What a hypocritical concern, considering she'd never invited me to join her either.

Avarium continued. "Have you been having nightmares?"

I froze at the jarring change of topic.

"I woke up a few times, because you—"

"No. I can be a sleep-talker though. Must be that."

"Okay, Evaris." She didn't sound convinced. "I'm going to sleep now. Goodnight."

An abrupt close to our conversation. That seemed to be a pattern.

"Goodnight," I replied, knowing I wouldn't have a good night myself.

CHAPTER 4

WORRYBUG

Day 9 | 20 trainees remaining

♫ SAID LIKE A POET - THEO BLEAK ♫

Cal Avarium kept me up at night. Mind you, I wasn't the only one with this problem. Boa complained that his roommate talked too much and snored too hard. Silver complained that his roommate burned lanterns and turned pages into the early hours of the morning. I did not, however, complain that my roommate snuck into my dreams and turned them into nightmares.

For the eighth night in a row, my silk pajamas and satin bedsheets lured me into Starsilk, Uncle Corvain's shop. The light filtered through strips of fabric over the windows, filling the room with a rainbow haze. My hands rifled through long, hanging swatches of endless colors and textures.

I had visited Starsilk plenty before this little dream of mine. It was the primary place my parents sourced fabrics from for client work. Once, though, my father had brought me here hoping my preference for plain clothes meant I might enjoy stitching up suits, if not ballgowns. I had picked out a solid purple velvet, which I made into bookskins instead. I loved dressing my novels in the same way Mother marveled at the gowns she made for me. But Father wasn't pleased, and I woke up one morning to find my books naked again.

Uncle Corvain understood my struggle. He also lacked interest in our family's line of work. That's why he ran this shop.

"There is business in everything, Ev," he told me once. *"You have the practical eye for it. I can tell."*

When I was twelve, Uncle Corvain and I traveled by horseback to his silkworm farm in the small town of Nominner. I spent three weeks dressed in scratchy clothes, boiling worms after they formed cocoons so I could harvest their silk. Once, I saved a cocoon in my pocket to see what it would look like if it survived. It produced a fuzzy brown moth with big black eyes, and it clung to my finger like a friend. It didn't know what I had done to the others.

Uncle Corvain entered from the back room. "Is that my favorite niece?"

"It's your favorite disappointment," I replied.

"Come here, you!" He laughed and opened his arms.

I flung myself into his embrace.

"You are no disappointment, Ev. You are *unshakable.*"

The Starfalls used that word a lot. I never really got what it meant.

Uncle Corvain pulled away, his eyes shimmering in the warm light. Outside of this dream, I hadn't spoken to him in months. He'd never disapproved of my training for the Academy, though he hadn't encouraged my act of rebellion either. What did he think of me making it this far? Had I become a disappointment to the one Starfall who had never called me such?

He reached for my head, and I chuckled. He always ruffled my hair, ever since I was little, though I'd grown too old for it now.

But instead, his fingers looped around my neck and squeezed.

My eyes widened. I gripped his hands, but they were too strong, no matter how hard I pried.

When I looked back up, Uncle Corvain was gone, replaced by the tall figure of Cal Avarium. Her clothes were dripping wet, her hair tangled with thorns and weeds.

"I heard someone tried to drown her, and she crawled out of the lake twenty minutes later."

I shot up in bed, gasping, my fingers feeling for my neck, but there were no hands wrapped around it.

My eyes darted across the room, where Avarium stirred under her blankets. I knew it was irrational, but I imagined that she'd tried to kill me just now—that she'd crawled back into bed right before I opened my eyes.

I gripped my sheets, struggling to steady my breath. I couldn't afford to keep having these nightmares. They left me in a state of total exhaustion and irritability. My outbursts against Professor Embre and Silver had proven this. After all the hard work I'd put into getting selected, how could I throw away my one shot to forge a path for myself?

Avarium's body stilled.

I sighed, loosening my grip on the sheets. I couldn't avoid Avarium when I shared a quarter with her, but maybe I didn't *need* to sleep in Room 4.

Heel to toe... I crept to the door. *Knees bent...*

I stepped into the lobby, barefoot in my golden pajamas. It was brighter here, the walls lit with mounted torches. I used one to light a handheld lantern someone had left lying around.

The library was on the third floor, across from the lecture hall. My lantern guided me up the staircase toward it. Books had always brought me comfort—perhaps being surrounded by them for a night could ward off my nightmares.

My eyes widened as I stepped off the landing. The library door was open, and inside, Boa sat at a wooden table, reading under the light of a handheld lantern. He was still in his trainee uniform, meaning he hadn't slept at all tonight.

I lurked a moment longer. Boa nearly turned a page, but his face hardened, and he craned his neck enough to glimpse me. In a single heartbeat, he jumped to his feet, gasping and staggering back.

"Whoa, whoa." I stepped inside, raising the lantern to my face. "Relax!"

His shoulders slumped forward with a sigh. "You scared me."

"Clearly. What did you think I was? A monster?"

"Worse." His lips curved into a subtle grin. "Professor Embre."

I laughed.

"You couldn't sleep either?" he asked.

"I wake up early."

He read the wall clock. "You normally wake up at 3:00?"

I shrugged. "If I'm stressed." Which, in truth, was every night.

I waited for him to question the cause of my stress, but he stepped down an aisle of bookshelves instead. I likely wouldn't have answered honestly, but his lack of curiosity stung a little.

"Are you reading more guardian memoirs?" I called as I crossed the room.

"What else would I be reading?"

I joined him in the aisle. He ran his fingers along a row of spines and pulled out a book that caught his eye.

"Sometimes the authors mention bits and pieces about their time at the Academy," he explained. "If I read enough of them, maybe I can piece together what the filtrations will be."

My jaw dropped. I had assumed he found these memoirs inspiring, not that he was searching for clues.

He flipped a page in the book he'd grabbed. "Genius, right?"

"More like *paranoid*, Boa. They have different filtrations for every group."

"No way. Think of the effort that would take. I've already noticed patterns—it seems like they have different filtration sets and cycle through them." He crossed his fingers. "We can only hope, right?"

I laughed in his face. "It's already hard enough to keep up with the program, and you're trying to get ahead?"

"Well, of course." Boa handed me the book, and I took it instinctively. "No one in town thought I'd get selected. Not even my parents. They said I'm too jumpy, too much of a worrybug. And now that I'm here and proved them wrong, I want to *keep* proving them wrong. It's precisely my forward-thinking that'll get me to the final five."

"*Worrybug*." I smiled at the dusty journal he handed me. "You're from Nominner."

Boa knelt by a lower shelf and scanned the titles, smiling all the more. "How do you recognize our town lingo?" It seemed I'd impressed him by putting the pieces together.

"I spent some time in Nominner."

"Really? There's nothing but meadows and fields and farms."

"It was for a summer apprenticeship. And that's what people called me there. A worrybug." *Because I hated boiling those cocoons.*

Boa pulled out a few more books. Perhaps he was debating whether to ask why a City girl would have an apprenticeship in a town like his. I was gearing up to tell him all about Uncle Corvain's business.

Instead, he took the books to the nearest table and motioned for me to come along. I sat across from him and dove into the memoir he'd passed me, but I could hardly pay attention. I wanted to tell him I understood the pressure he was under. There were people I'd proven wrong too, that I wanted to *keep* proving wrong. We could prove everyone wrong together, as allies in the program. Hell, we could *win* together.

But I said none of this because he hadn't shown even a little interest in my background. Maybe I could validate opening up a little, if only he would ask the bare minimum: *Why are you in the library so late?*

He didn't, though. They never did. No one put in the work to truly know me.

I pursed my lips, frowning at the pages I'd given up on reading. Finding an opportunity to talk about my home life was the least of my worries right now. I needed to deal with these nightmares, and while sleeping in the library could be a quick fix, I couldn't avoid my roommate forever.

Perhaps I needed to ask the question I'd been avoiding all week. The answer would either fix my problem or make it worse, but at this point, I needed to take that leap.

"Hey." I looked up, my voice quiet. "Could I ask you something?"

He peered over his pages and waited.

"Do you know *why* she killed that boy?"

Boa's expression darkened as he looked away from our lanterns, casting his face in shadow. I didn't need to say Avarium's name for him to know exactly who I was talking about.

"His name was Chima. According to the article, he'd been bullying Avarium for quite some time, but she always ignored him. Never snapped.

So, to push her over the edge, he went to the woods where her little brother was playing hide-and-seek with his friends. Then he caught him and held a knife to his throat."

My frown loosened. "So she killed Chima to protect her brother?"

"That's why the article was titled, *The Belladonna Savior*. The guardians thought her heroism could be of use to the Force."

My face flushed hot. I was an only child, but I could imagine that if I *had* a sibling, I would do anything to protect them. If I'd known Avarium's motives earlier, perhaps I wouldn't be having this nightmare. Why the hell would these boys twist her story like that?

Boa read the frustration on my face. "It's not crazy that she killed him, Evaris. It's *how* she killed him."

"They were in the woods, and Chima had a knife," I argued. "She had to use *something*, right? What else could she find but a log?"

Boa leaned in and whispered, "I heard she kept hitting him, even after he was already dead."

I was hesitant to believe another rumor.

"Look. I don't blame the guardians one bit for selecting her," he continued. "But imagine if she cares about making the top five just as much as she cares about her brother. Who's to say she wouldn't kill to win?"

The morning bell tolled.

I woke up alone in the library with a blanket draped over me.

Boa must have brought it from his quarter.

As I passed Gup in the lecture hall, he flashed a smile that I didn't reciprocate. The stitches on his uniform were thick and drew attention from the other boys, who whispered and glanced my way. It occurred to me that even if he hadn't said a word, they would assume I'd been the one to help. Who else at the Academy had a sewing background?

The rumor didn't bother me as much as I'd expected, which I attributed to finally having a few hours of decent rest. The nightmare hadn't come back. Perhaps because I'd slept away from Avarium, or perhaps because I'd learned the truth about the boy she'd murdered. Either way, I felt prepared to face whatever the program planned to throw at me today.

I took my seat next to Boa. He whispered, "Was it you?"

"No," I said, loud enough for any speculating boys to overhear me. Then, quieter, I muttered, "Thanks for the blanket."

Boa kept tapping his pencil against our shared desk. "What blanket?"

I squinted, believing he was joking, but he didn't crack. Had he forgotten? No, who could forget going downstairs to fetch a blanket, coming up to deliver it, and going down once more to sleep?

"Boa, stop that," Professor Embre said.

He gulped and set his pencil down. "Sorry, Professor."

She stared a moment longer before holding up a stack of papers—the written assignments we'd turned in two days ago. We had each crafted an essay on a topic of choice related to the Underground, the organization that had tormented the Vakoi Empire for years. I had written about the raids on our towns, an offense that had always shaken me. I was a little girl when I heard about them storming into homes and gouging out eyes. The Force had kept the Underground under control since then. Eradicating them was their next problem—one I would hopefully help with as a guardian myself.

"I graded your papers," Professor Embre said ominously.

Boa almost picked up his pencil again, but then remembered her scolding. He fidgeted with his hands instead. It was like he sensed that something different was about to happen.

Professor Embre confirmed his worst-case scenario: "The trainee with the lowest score goes home."

Goosebumps ran up my arms. *Our first filtration.* We hadn't even known it was a test until it was too late.

Silver looked over his shoulder and made eye contact. He seemed more concerned about me than frustrated about our argument last night. I was still beneath him, in his eyes, and while I could own that with Defense training, it disturbed me that he questioned my intellect. It felt like I was back at home again, with the people around me doubting that I could reach my goals.

I narrowed my eyes at Professor Embre as she cleared her throat, about to announce the filtered trainee.

Please don't be me.

She locked eyes with a trainee in the back row and called a name that wasn't mine.

Boa and I sighed in unison. Silver ran his hands through his hair in relief.

The filtered boy's name was such a cursed sound, as it came with a cursed fate. I would likely forget his name in a few days, but I would never forget the twisted look on his face when he walked down the aisle, heading for the door Professor Embre held open for him.

He stopped and looked back at the nineteen of us that remained. It was dead quiet.

"A guardian is waiting in the courtyard to escort you home," Professor Embre said.

He lowered his head and walked out.

To my surprise, Avarium glared at the door he vanished through. I couldn't place why she'd care.

"Daxel?" Professor Embre called.

The boy in the patchy uniform sat up straight.

"Yes, Professor?" Gup replied, his voice breaking.

"Congratulations. You got the highest score."

That afternoon, Commander Roz had us train with daggers for the first time. Every guardian carried one in their overcoat, he explained, no matter their primary tool or division placement. Plus, if you could fight with a dagger, you could fight with almost anything—a knife, a sharpened stick, whatever you had.

With nineteen of us left, there could only be nine pairs. I was the last trainee standing after Commander Roz assigned partners. Everyone started without me, practicing the blade strikes and blocks he'd demonstrated.

"I'll be working with you, Evaris." His tone was softer than usual. Perhaps Commander Roz pitied me for how much I'd been struggling, but I set my bitterness aside and embraced the rare opportunity for one-on-one instruction. It was easier to learn from him directly than floundering through the moves with a fellow trainee.

With his guidance, my motions flowed.

I blocked a swipe, my dagger clashing against his.

"Good," he said.

About ten minutes later, Commander Roz left me to make his rounds and critique the others. I cut the air, facing an invisible opponent. But every so often, I'd lose focus and peek at Avarium.

Commander Roz had paired her with Gup, and their breakneck speed drew glances from other trainees too. Eventually, one of them would misstep and stab the other in the chest, right?

We stared, waiting for a calamity.

But they fought in perfect harmony.

CHAPTER 5

LABRAT

Day 10 | 19 trainees remaining

♫ IS IT FADING? - RIZZERS ♫

Cal Avarium got... flowers.

Dead ones, but they were flowers nonetheless, and treated as such. Someone had left a bouquet of them by Room 4, along with a little note that read, *FOR AVARIUM.*

It happened the day after Commander Roz paired her and Gup together in Defense class. Their perfect coordination had stolen the spotlight from the filtered trainee. No one even mentioned his cursed name during supper.

Today, Boa told me he'd be taking a nap during recreation time, so I read in the lobby instead of the dining hall. I'd only gotten through a chapter or two before Silver and the Miranda boys emerged from the staircase, sweaty and loud after their daily run.

Despite my presence, they sat on the sofas nearby to socialize. I feigned immersion in my novel to eavesdrop—it was rare that I could witness Silver interacting with them.

"5:32," said Krevall, referencing the little notepad where he tracked their run times. He pushed his glasses up and grinned at Silver. "If you were thirty-two seconds faster, you could've reached Avarium's record."

Make that thirty-four seconds faster, I corrected. Her real time, I'd heard, was 4:58.

"You should join us tomorrow," Silver said.

I turned a page, still pretending to read.

"Princess," he said. "I'm talking to *you*."

My eyes widened as I looked up. All four of them were staring. Had Silver really just invited me to join them on a group run? *Me*, the trainee with the slowest mile time, running with *them*, who were among the fastest?

Toll, Krevall, and Nash didn't smile, nod, or otherwise indicate a desire for me to say yes.

Well, that was fine by me. I was still riding on the embarrassment of that awful field class two days ago. Why humiliate myself further by falling behind in a group run too?

I stuck my nose back into my book. "I'll pass."

"Evaris," Silver said, almost pleading.

My grip on the pages tightened. I hadn't spoken privately with Silver since I'd blown up at him, and we still hadn't gone back to practicing in the courtyard either. Maybe he missed the satisfaction he got from being better than me during our training sessions, and that's why he invited me on a run. He knew I wouldn't keep up with them and was hungry for an ego boost.

"Avoiding your problems isn't gonna help," he added.

I slammed my book shut.

"Ooh!" Nash exclaimed, waving his stocky arms. "Better back off, Silver."

Krevall laughed. I would have found their humor infuriating, had Toll not distracted me. He hadn't been acting like himself these past couple of days. Maybe he hadn't lied to Gup—maybe someone had framed him as the uniform-cutter. While we hadn't verified the culprit, most boys settled on believing it was him. He'd been much nicer to his roommate ever since; not once had he flicked Gup's neck.

Toll fidgeted with a tin of feathered darts, his expression blank. He no longer resembled the cocky trainee who'd walked into the Academy with a gait that said, *You're beneath me.*

"Toll." I pointed at the tin of darts in his hands. "Mind if I use those?"

He shrugged and stood to walk the darts over. Krevall and Nash continued chatting with Silver.

Once Toll reached my sofa, I seized the opportunity.

"Let's play a game," I said. I never would've thought I'd ask to throw darts with the boy I'd once called *Neck Flicker.*

"Sure, okay."

We squared up, aiming darts at the cork targets on the lobby walls. Toll was an excellent shot, much better than I was. Sometimes I missed and pierced the wall by accident, adding wounds to the many others that past trainees had left before me.

"You look tired," I said.

Toll aimed another dart. "Yeah, well, aren't we all?"

He struck the red bullseye and faced me with a shrug like it meant nothing.

Footsteps echoed from the staircase, turning our heads.

Gup stepped off the landing wearing a new uniform set—the suture thread formed a different pattern. He shot me a quick smile and made a beeline for his quarter.

"Wait," Toll blurted.

Gup shuffled to a stop and looked over, brows raised.

"Do you wanna play darts with us?" Toll asked.

I couldn't believe it. The same trainee who had flicked his neck and called him *pretty boy* was now inviting him to a game.

After a moment of hesitation, Gup made his way to our side of the lobby. He had just plucked a dart from a tin when Room 4 swung open, and Avarium stepped out. Unlike Gup's entrance, hers silenced the room. Silver, Krevall, and Nash glued their lips and stared.

My roommate lingered in the doorway for an unsettling amount of time, eyes on the floor, hair falling in a way that obstructed her face. It took me a moment to realize that she wasn't acting defeated. She'd spotted something by her boots.

I squinted. A bundle of dead flowers lay outside our quarter. The rest of us had walked past it without noticing; we had no reason to look at the floor.

The last time I'd entered Room 4 was after lunch, when I'd stowed my book bag before our afternoon classes. Whoever had left those flowers must have done so in the past five or six hours.

Avarium picked up the bouquet. The dry flowers crinkled as she twisted them to read the note attached. A few petals broke and fluttered to the ground.

Nash laughed, soon followed by Krevall and Silver. Their eyes were not on Avarium, but on Gup. He'd sat with her during meals the past couple of days and was the closest thing she had to a friend right now.

Toll and I met eyes. Neither of us found this funny.

"Hey!" Gup's cheeks turned red. "You really think I'd give flowers to a girl like her?"

The boys stopped laughing, their wide eyes shooting in Avarium's direction.

Gup was the last to face her. As soon as they locked eyes, he darted down the staircase he'd come from.

Avarium glared in our direction, took her flowers in, and slammed the door.

It was quiet for a moment. Silver, Krevall, and Nash were looking at Toll now.

Nash broke into a smile. "How'd you come up with that one?"

Krevall laughed again. He reached under his glasses to wipe his eyes. Meanwhile, Silver looked guilty for having laughed at all.

Toll shook his head adamantly. "It wasn't me, okay?"

"Well, who else would have done it?" Nash asked.

Silver narrowed his eyes. "It wouldn't be the first time you made a fool of Gup."

"Are you serious?" Toll took a step toward them, raising his voice. "Honestly, by how little you trust me, I'm starting to think it might be one of *you*!"

Word spread fast about the flowers. The consensus was that Toll had planted them to humiliate his roommate. This worked in Gup's favor; no one believed he had a crush on Avarium. But even so, he sat alone during supper, instead of with her.

I returned to Room 4 that evening to find the bouquet sitting in a lantern. Avarium had removed the candle inside to make space for the stems. It was a makeshift vase, but it was pretty in its own right.

"You put them up," I noted.

Avarium shrugged. "I've never gotten flowers before."

They were dead, and she didn't care at all.

A few days later, it was Doctor Blimmery's turn to teach field class. We left the building to find him standing in the field beside a white horse. His dark overcoat flowed in the wind, and a bandolier of throwing blades glimmered across his chest.

"Looking classy with that steed, Doctor!" Nash yelled.

Doctor Blimmery's gray beard bounced as he laughed. "Why, thank you, Nash!" he shouted back. "Now Boa, where are you, kid?"

"Here!" Boa raised his hand.

"Would you assist me with some demonstrations?"

"Well, of course." Boa ran up to him and mounted the white horse in a single, fluid motion. As it turned out, Boa was a real horseman. Doctor Blimmery used him as a teacher's assistant to show us the basics.

Silver rolled his eyes a few times.

While Boa's skills surprised us, Doctor Blimmery had already known he was good with horses. The guardians had all kinds of notes on us, as they'd studied our academic, athletic, and social skills for months leading up to our selection. Perhaps Doctor Blimmery had even vouched for Boa himself. He clearly liked the boy. The thought made *me* roll my eyes this time.

Finally, it was our turn to give riding a shot. Doctor Blimmery led us to the stable across the field, which stored even more horses. He brought another one out and placed its lead rope in my hands.

"He's a nice fellow," Doctor Blimmery whispered.

It was a striking white horse. Well, they all were. Only guardians had white horses.

"See this mark, kids?" He spoke louder, addressing everyone, and pointed to the four-petaled flower emblem branded on my horse's shoulder. It matched the mark branded on Doctor Blimmery's forehead—every guardian in the Force had one. I would too, someday, if I were lucky.

"Right under the emblem are two numbers. The first is its identification number, and the second is its birthday. Note that its *fifteenth* birthday is just two weeks from now. Since each horse works for exactly fifteen years, that's also its retirement date."

I frowned. While whispering to me a moment ago, Doctor Blimmery had referred to my horse as *he*. But to the class, he had used *it*.

Krevall adjusted his glasses. "What happens after its retirement?"

"Nothing, I'm afraid," Doctor Blimmery replied, leaving us to fill in the gap. His eyes met mine, and I scowled, realizing exactly what he was doing.

We were distant relatives, Doctor Blimmery and I. My mother's maiden name, Owding, matched his current one. She had come from a family of authors and married into a family of fashion designers. I often felt like I was born on the wrong side.

Doctor Blimmery had likely heard about my time at Uncle Corvain's farm in Nominner, and how I'd struggled to boil those silkworms. Now he wanted to use my soft spot for creatures against me by sowing my sympathy for this horse, which was scheduled to die within a month.

As if I would filter myself over something that trivial. *You're not getting rid of me that easily, Doctor.*

"Sounds about right." My grip on the lead rope tightened. "Horses leave their prime after fifteen years. There's no room for mediocrity in the Force."

I am not mediocre.

A look of disappointment crossed his face. "No, there isn't, is there?"

The following morning, Doctor Blimmery pushed a metal cart into the dining hall. It contained nineteen glasses of beet juice, one for each of us. Which was odd, considering it was breakfast; we normally drank beet juice with lunch.

"Guess what, kids?" His voice echoed in the vast room. "You finally have a day off!"

We sighed in unison. Well, except Boa.

"Do you hear that?" he whispered.

I listened, picking up on the faint sound of footsteps coming from the common room.

"Backup doctors from Vakoi City Hospital." Boa smiled as if it were a birthday present. "Today they're poisoning our juice."

A look of realization crossed Silver's face. "Well, I'm sure knowing in advance has helped you *loads*." Despite his mockery, I could tell Boa had slightly impressed him. And had maybe even made him nervous too. Silver's leg bounced under the table.

Doctor Blimmery passed out our laced beet juice, his cart creaking as he wheeled it from table to table. He gave us a rundown on the belladonna plant and how guardians laced their tools with its extracted serum. As a precaution against a guardian's own tools being used against them, every member of the Force went through tolerance training in the program—a slow process of gaining immunity to their own poison.

As he explained this, three more guardians entered the dining hall. I identified them as members of the Medical Division by the badges on their shoulders, which matched Doctor Blimmery's. They waved, and that's when the unease spread from our table to the rest of them.

"Now, I should warn you—this won't be an easy process," Doctor Blimmery continued. "We'll need to take it slowly, so your juice won't always have belladonna serum in it. Every day, I recommend seeing if you can detect its slightly sweet undertone, as you may be tested on this at a later date."

Boa whipped out a notebook and jotted down the hint.

Slightly sweet, he wrote on one line. *Belladonna detection filtration confirmed,* he wrote on another.

"Can you show me that later?" Silver asked. For once, he didn't assume Boa was over-preparing.

Boa grinned. "You're always welcome to look at my notes, Silver. I show

Evaris all the time."

Silver raised a brow at me. "Oh, does he?"

Maybe it bothered him that I'd been taking help from Boa, yet still hadn't shown up to train with him in the courtyard like we used to. It'd been a week since our last session. I'd considered bringing it up a few times, but after his smug reaction just now, I felt less inclined.

If you resent me so much, go sit with your Miranda friends.

Doctor Blimmery reached our table next and set a glass by my tray. "Here you are, Ev."

I froze. Only family called me *Ev*, and I wondered if he used the nickname so my fellow trainees would speculate about my relationship to him. If word spread about us being distant relatives, they might assume I got into the program out of privilege, which couldn't be further from the truth.

If anything, Doctor Blimmery had vouched against me. He had taken me to supper a few months ago to convince me to flunk my exams and run slower than I could during my school's physical evaluations. The fact that he wanted me to self-sabotage only proved I was on the right track. He wouldn't have interfered if I hadn't stood a chance.

Looking back on it now, he had likely caught wind that Professor Embre had her eyes on me.

Doctor Blimmery clapped once. "Alright, let's taste it!"

Every trainee had a glass now, but no one jumped at the opportunity to take the first sip. It was rather intimidating, considering how three Medical guardians stood along the wall, staring us down, white briefcases at the ready.

"It must be bad if we need *them*," Silver said, gesturing with his eyes.

"It's the one filtration that seems to be repeated every year without fail," Boa explained in a hushed tone. "The guardians are here to administer something called antiserum. It makes you throw up to get the poison out of your system. Only take it if you're certain you're about to pass out."

I frowned. "Why?"

"If you throw up, your body will absorb less belladonna—and you can only build immunity to however much you absorb. So... you'll fall behind in tolerance training."

Silver gulped. "And if you *do* pass out?"

"You *won't* be able to take the antiserum," Boa answered. "You'd have to get transferred to Vakoi City Hospital for more intensive treatment. Which would automatically filter you. It usually happens to two or three trainees per cycle."

"That many?" I exclaimed.

Slowly, trainees began to raise their glasses. And slowly, trainees began to react.

I took a few small sips, and my hands began to shake almost instantly. With another gulp, my head started spinning on a swivel. At least it felt like it. I couldn't lock eyes with Boa and Silver no matter how hard I tried. I was sweating. The room was hot. I was going to be hospitalized, wasn't I? My body wasn't strong enough to stay conscious, and by passing out, I'd get myself filtered.

I heard boys scrambling, their shouts blurring into a rumbly, incoherent drum. I resisted the urge to follow their lead and physically run from my symptoms.

To ground myself, I leaned over and pressed my forehead onto the dining table. I gripped the edge as if my life depended on it—as though falling out of my chair meant I was toppling off a cliff.

"Evaris!" called a voice I couldn't identify. It was louder than the others. *Closer.*

"Stay with me," he continued. Or maybe it was a separate person speaking now. I was too focused on tightening my grip on the table to tell. I was too high up. If I fell, I'd *splat* right onto the sharp rocks below.

My hands turned numb from the pressure of my grip. Despite exerting all my strength, my fingers unraveled against my will. I sailed down, trying to scream, but no sounds came out.

And right before I hit those piercing rocks, two hands reached for me.

I fell right into them.

There were more voices now, speaking words I couldn't make out. I heard a boy my age say something over and over—something that felt like a plea—and before I knew it, the voice began to fade.

"Please." It was barely a whisper. "Please... mouth... open..."

Perhaps I misinterpreted the request, but I'd try anything to keep from passing out. I used the last of my strength to open my mouth.

"Drink," the voice said.

I obeyed, swallowing the most vile, sour fluid I had ever tasted in my life. It was so horrid that my body surged upright, tearing through my immense fatigue. The person who had caught me scrambled away.

And before I knew it, I was vomiting my breakfast across the marble floor—along with a yellow liquid. It matched the color of the antiserum vials around the room, held by the backup Medical guardians. One of them knelt beside me, his vial empty. I had drunk it entirely.

This was not the worst-case scenario. I hadn't passed out from the poison, but as Boa had explained, I hadn't fully absorbed it either. The next dose would be stronger and hit me harder.

My eyes burned. Classes were challenging enough as is. The last thing I needed was another sector to fall behind in. I wiped my face dry before the tears could fall.

Boa and Silver appeared in my clearing vision, relieved that I was still conscious.

And I wondered, as they helped me to my feet, which one of them had saved me.

CHAPTER 6

BLOODHOUND

Day 15 | 17 trainees remaining

Cal Avarium didn't kill me. That was the first thought that came to mind when I woke from my post-dose *nap*, which had turned into more of a deep sleep. Thanks to the belladonna toxins in my system, my head ached with a fury, my eyes glued themselves shut, and the exhaustion pinned me to my sweaty sheets. I was more vulnerable than ever, yet Avarium hadn't taken the opportunity to strike.

My logical side didn't believe she would've done so, of course. But my smaller, irrational side still felt the horror of that old nightmare.

I fought the tiredness in my arms to rub my eyes. I could barely keep them open for more than a few seconds before they drifted shut. With some time and focus, I managed to force them wide for a bit longer and even push myself into a seated position.

The sun was setting, casting Room 4 in an orange glow. The fact that I'd slept through the entire day made me chuckle. Why had the guardians called it a *day off* in the first place, if they had known we'd spend it sick?

Boa's prediction earlier had been spot-on. Before I'd gone to sleep, Doctor Blimmery had announced that two trainees were transferred to Vakoi City Hospital. They had passed out before taking the antiserum, which meant they required an injection of calabar serum—belladonna's antidote. Upon full recovery, they'd be sent home, filtered from the program.

It's a miracle that I'm still here.

I glanced at the paper on my nightstand. Doctor Blimmery had given us each a page with two lists of symptoms—the left labeled *PANIC* and the right labeled *DON'T*. Apparently, it was common for trainees to knock on his door in the middle of the night.

"Unless your symptoms are in the panic category, don't wake me up," he'd said. *"I have enough trouble sleeping as is."*

Since I wasn't hyperventilating, feeling frigid, or experiencing any of the other symptoms on the *PANIC* side of the page, I stayed relatively calm that evening.

That is, until I spotted Avarium across the room, still in bed.

Motionless.

I pulled myself free from under my blankets and nearly lost balance when I tried to stand. I gripped my nightstand to steady myself.

"Avarium," I choked out, letting go to test whether I could stay on my feet. I was surprisingly stable, but my blurry vision left me wobbling anyway.

I sloppily crossed the room and reached her bedside.

Her skin was deathly pale.

My eyes widened. What if she'd experienced a delayed reaction to the toxins? What if she had cried for help with what little voice she had left, and I had slept right through it?

I grabbed her shoulder and shook. "Avarium!"

She shuffled, slightly, her eyes fluttering open. After a few blinks, the realization set in.

Avarium shot up, her eyes widening, her breaths short. "Am I late?"

I shook my head. "It's our day off, remember?"

She stumbled out of bed as though my statement offered no reprieve. The mere momentum nearly sent her falling, but I caught her by the waist and waited until she met my gaze.

"Relax, okay? There's nothing scheduled."

Avarium broke free from my grip and opened her drawer, from which she produced a silver stopwatch. She paused to flip it over in her hand.

"It's the only thing you brought with you," I noted. "Is it special?"

"Yes." She tucked the stopwatch into her pocket.

"How so?"

"It's the reason I'm here."

In a flash, Avarium was at the door, rushing to go *somewhere* to do *something*—both of which I had no clue. She nearly stepped out, but hesitated to peer back at me.

"Thanks for waking me up, Evaris."

Before I could reply, she disappeared.

Our schedule resumed the next day, even though I hadn't returned to normal. My mind was foggy; it was even harder than usual to stay focused during Research class. Boa kept tapping my notebook with his pencil, which made my blood boil. I plucked it from his hand and scribbled until the charcoal tip turned round. He hated writing with dull pencils.

"Sorry about that," I said after class.

By lunch, I felt more like myself, but the sight of beet juice coated my tongue with a bitter taste. "It better not be laced."

"I don't think it is." Boa smacked his lips. "It was a little sweeter yesterday, don't you think?"

"Can't remember." Silver met my gaze before taking a sip. He swallowed hard and hesitated before speaking again. "So, Evaris... have you been sleeping any better?"

I frowned. "What?"

"Well, you were passed out in the library the other night. Boa said you were stressed."

My cheeks flushed hot. *So it was Silver who brought me that blanket.*

"I'm fine now," I muttered, lowering my head. What if I was wrong about him? What if he wasn't just helping me for the ego boost?

I held my glass and tapped my index finger against it. Once. Twice. A third time. "Do you think we could maybe... meet at the courtyard later, at the usual time?"

When I looked back up, Silver smiled with his crooked teeth.

"Sure thing, Evaris."

My body fought against me during Defense class that afternoon. Whenever I moved, my vision lagged—which was extra unsettling when a fellow trainee was coming at me with a dagger.

I winced and raised my tool. Miraculously, it blocked the incoming strike just in time.

"Let's take a water break," Gup said. I could tell from the look on his face that the break was for *me*, not him.

I applied more pressure to our crossed blades. "I'm fine."

"Come on." He redirected my dagger away with a swing of his arm. "I'm worried you might impale me."

"What does it matter? I could stitch you right back up." The words came out like an insult, but he laughed as though I'd made a joke.

"Evaris!" Commander Roz appeared beside us out of thin air. *Guardians and their ghostly feet.*

I straightened up. "Yes, Commander?"

"You'll work with Krevall for the rest of class. Daxel, you're with Nash."

Gup leaned toward Commander Roz and whispered, "She's a bit tipsy."

I glared at him, and he rushed off toward his new partner.

"You're not the only one, Evaris." Commander Roz patted my shoulder before walking off.

A moment later, Krevall approached with a dagger in hand. "Go easy on me, Starfall. My eyes aren't sharp today." He tapped his blade against the frame of his glasses. "Not that they're any good to begin with. These stupid things."

I smiled a little. It was nice to know I wasn't the only one struggling with the poison.

I met Silver in the courtyard about an hour after supper. He ran through hand-to-hand combat drills with me—no daggers. I needed to get back to the basics, which I still hadn't nailed.

"Need a break?"

Normally, I'd say yes whenever he offered. This time, I shook my head. Only when I could barely breathe did I finally drop to the ground, giving my sore legs a break.

Silver was right. If I wanted a real shot at making the final five, I needed to push myself to my limit more often.

I looked up at him, breathless. "Why are you helping me?"

He shrugged. "I think it'd be nice to win with you."

I searched his face. "Is it really that simple?"

He raised his brows. "Does it need to be complicated?"

After showering off, I slipped into bed and hesitated to reach for a novel. I wasn't in the mood—the Academy and its inhabitants were unusually comforting tonight.

Instead, I peered across the quarter at Avarium, who was doing her nightly stretches. The lantern on her desk held that same mysterious bouquet. The flowers were still dead. They hadn't lost any value to her.

"Any idea who gave those to you?"

Avarium folded an arm, stretching her shoulder out. "No."

"Gup, maybe?" He'd been avoiding her for close to a week now. They'd gone back to eating separately—and while Commander Roz had paired them together a few more times during classes, they were never in sync again.

"Someone else, I'm sure." She stopped stretching and got into bed. "Goodnight, Evaris."

A jarring exit, as usual.

I chuckled and laid my head back. "Goodnight, Avarium."

Our conversation had gone nowhere, and yet it felt like it had gone *somewhere*. I even wished it could've lasted longer. Now that my roommate didn't seem quite so terrifying, I wanted to know about her little brother and the bully she'd killed. I figured that maybe, just *maybe*, I shouldn't be so adamant about keeping my distance. We were the only girls at the Academy. *Perhaps we ought to stick together.*

Life must've been playing a sick game with me, because the next morning, Professor Embre ordered us to split into pairs for a Research assignment.

Boa turned to me instinctively, and I nodded in confirmation. We were desk partners; it was the obvious choice. I looked over to see that Silver had partnered with Krevall.

With seventeen of us remaining, Avarium was the odd one out. She looked around, but where her eyes went, trainees looked away. Even Gup had a partner.

Professor Embre's bug eyes searched the room, much to the same result. "Would anyone like to bring Cal in for a group of three?"

A pit formed in my stomach. Under any other circumstances, I would've raised my hand and said, *We will, Professor!*

But in a program like this, I couldn't afford to be nice at the cost of my reputation.

I continued to divert my gaze.

"Very well," Professor Embre said. "Cal?"

"Yes, Professor?"

"You'll work alone."

It took her twice as long to finish the assignment.

Two days later, I woke up feeling normal. No headache, no foggy vision, no ringing in my ears...

Perhaps I even felt *better* than normal. I hadn't experienced that nightmare since our first belladonna dose. Sleeping straight until morning was a luxury my younger self had taken for granted.

During field class that day, Silver requested we pair up. Professor Embre had us practicing horseback formations again, and according to Silver, Boa was getting even more cocky, though rightfully so. He deserved to work with Nash, a more equal pair. They could push each other better.

"Plus," Silver said, "I have some top-secret information to share."

"Of course. You and your big mouth." I mounted my horse and gave its neck a pat. It was the same old soul I'd been working with since the beginning. I would miss it next month after its retirement on its fifteenth birthday. Doctor Blimmery said I could be there to say goodbye.

Silver pulled his horse up next to mine, and we rode side by side toward the opposite end of the field.

"You know, you play hard to get, Princess, but I know you love gossip as much as I do. Isn't that all you people do at those balls and galas and what-not?"

I rolled my eyes. "Just tell me already."

He grinned with his big teeth and leaned toward me. "Toll's been getting death threats from Avarium."

"*What*?" I tightened the reins too hard, and my horse tossed his head in protest.

"We were studying in the library this morning, and he told me everything. Apparently, the notes started after she gave herself those flowers. She's been slipping them under his door."

I resisted the urge to trot away, right out of this conversation. Rumors about the uniform-cutter and the flower-giver had never stopped circulating. Accusations had initially settled on Toll before shifting to Avarium. It was ridiculous how quickly they believed she had gifted herself flowers, yet no one could give me a better description of her motive than, *Your roommate is crazy.*

When I looked back at Silver, his face had paled.

"You look sick, all of a sudden."

He made eye contact and blinked. "Huh?"

"Oh, come on. You know you can't keep secrets. They slip right between your big buck teeth."

Normally he'd laugh, but he diverted his gaze, quiet. I'd never seen him hesitate to gossip before.

Finally, he exhaled a heavy breath. "You won't tell her, right?"

I frowned. "Who? Avarium?"

He nodded.

"It's not like she's my friend."

"But—"

"Just spit it!"

"Fine!" He stopped his horse at the end of the field, as did I. We were a bit farther from everyone as we awaited our turn to practice today's formation. Even so, Silver lowered his voice. "Toll wants to kill one of the horses, and frame Avarium for it."

My jaw dropped. "You're joking."

"Dead serious. He wants her gone before she acts on her threats."

"Silver, she's *not* sending him threats, okay? It's gotta be someone else."

"And how are you so sure?"

He wouldn't take the lack of my nightmares as proof of her innocence, nor the fact that she cherished her flowers. And I didn't want to give the impression that I was friends with her—Silver's big mouth would spread the word, and I'd be the next trainee people kept their distance from. So I dodged the question instead. "Just talk some sense into Toll, will you? If his idea backfires, he could get into serious trouble. These horses are property of the Force."

"No way. If Toll wants to lighten the competition and better my odds, I'm not gonna stop him."

"Evaris! Silver!" Professor Embre's voice boomed from across the field.

Our backs straightened as she blew into a golden whistle, and my worries about Toll and Avarium temporarily vanished.

Silver and I met eyes, nodding. We whipped our reins in unison, shooting across the field, weaving our horses left and right in a chaotic pattern. If a member of the Underground with a long-range tool were to try to shoot us down, it'd be impossible to predict our movements.

When we reached Professor Embre's side of the field, we stopped our horses next to each other and caught our breaths.

She clicked a button on her stopwatch, checked the time, and looked back up with her creepily wide eyes. "Five seconds too slow. Try again."

We frowned and followed another failed pair of trainees heading back. We would try again, and again, until we'd finally get it right.

Avarium and her reluctant partner, Gup, had been the first to reach our target time. They sat on the front steps of the Academy, chatting together. Gup laughed at something Avarium said, dropping his smile once he noticed I was watching.

A few days later, our lunch juice contained belladonna again. Boa insisted he could tell, but no one believed him.

Every day since our first dose last week, at least one trainee would insist our juice was laced. We always drank our glasses in full to keep up with tolerance training, in case it was, but the side effects never came.

Until today, when Doctor Blimmery waltzed into the dining hall with a wooden crate, confirming Boa's suspicion. Inside were a dozen vials of yellow antiserum.

"This is the last time you'll get a warning, kids. From now on, the box stays here, laced or not." He slipped it under the serving table and left as quickly as he'd come.

I should've felt optimistic that there weren't Medical guardians on standby—our instructors didn't expect our reactions to be as risky. Still, my hands were shaking before I took a sip. I folded them under the table as Boa and Silver stared me down, their lips forming flat lines. They knew this might be my last day too.

Would I miss them? Likely, but not because we were friends. Whether it was to better our odds or boost our morale, we were just using each other. But I would miss what they represented—camaraderie toward a shared goal.

I never had this before.

Silver forced a grin. "Don't be stressed." It was stupid advice, considering my reaction to the last dose. If I wanted to catch up in tolerance training, I needed to fully absorb the toxins this time. I couldn't take the antiserum. This would be a true test of whether I could handle the Academy.

Boa held my gaze, his expression sharpening. It meant something—his choice to stay quiet. He didn't intend to tell me what I wanted to hear.

I took a deep breath and grabbed my glass. The familiar sound of mumbling voices and uneven footsteps echoed around me as boys began to react.

The swirling fluid in my glass made me think of how sick it'd made me last time.

Silver raised his juice for a toast. "Cheers to the best Starfall."

I offered a trembling smile. It was a nice maybe-farewell.

Boa lifted his juice in response. "To Evaris."

And with that, I took a sip.

CHAPTER 7

HORSEMAN

Day 23 | 17 trainees remaining

♫ THE DEVIL · SARAH ♫

Cal Avarium could be nice sometimes. She proved this the day after our second dose.

My nausea was unmatched. I could hardly walk, could hardly see… Reading in bed was impossible, so I spent most of the time blinking at the ceiling, feeling sorry for myself. I saved every last bit of energy for the expeditions to and from the restroom because I sure as hell wasn't going to let anyone carry me in and out.

After Medical class—which I'd missed, of course—Doctor Blimmery brought me a bowl of black oatmeal. Yes, *black*.

"Looks like literal excrement," I said.

"You're funny, you." He handed me the bowl. "It contains activated charcoal to help with your recovery. But if it's too gross, you don't have to eat it."

I assumed he was obligated to bring me medicine but hoped I wouldn't take it. While he didn't want me here, I was no ordinary Starfall, just as he was no ordinary Owding. I had earned my spot, whether he liked it or not.

I took a bite immediately.

Then he left, and after eating every morsel of that oatmeal, I continued lying there, battling my eyes to read a book. The words kept overlapping or flipping upside down, forming a puzzle I had to really focus on to solve. It took me half an hour to get through one paragraph, which resulted in a massive headache.

I went back to observing the four-petaled flower designs on the ceiling. Someone, at some point, had painted those marks up there. I wondered what their story was.

And I wondered when I would have water. For the glory of Vakoi, I was *thirsty*.

It must have been recreation time when Avarium returned to Room 4 and sat on her bed. She watched me for a while without trying to hide it. I pretended not to care, but my heart was pounding against my ribcage. If she was going to strangle me to death, it would be now, at my most vulnerable.

I shook the thought away. I was over being irrationally terrified of her.

Despite this, I flinched when she finally stood and crept to my bedside. She hovered so close that her black hair brushed my cheek. I was paralyzed, and the fear made me dizzy. Her head started spinning in circles.

It's just the belladonna, I told myself.

I closed my eyes at the sound of a *click*, and when I gathered the courage to open them, she was gone, walking away. On my nightstand, she'd placed a steel canister—the kind cleaners took swigs from while sweeping the halls or dusting the rooms. Outside of Defense classes, trainees only had access to cups by the dispensers downstairs.

My heart settled, and the thought of water made me remember my parched tongue. I shuffled up in bed and reached for the canister.

"Where did you get this?"

"I stole it from the kitchen," Avarium answered, already halfway to our restroom. She shut the door behind her and started the shower.

She was no conversationalist.

I downed the rest of the water she'd brought me.

By my third evening, I started to gain some strength back. And I could read again. Slowly, but gratefully. Finally, something to do.

I had just finished two chapters of what felt like the most exciting story ever when someone knocked on the door.

"Come in!"

It was Boa. "Hey. Heard you're feeling better."

"A bit."

"You up for a walk?"

I looked at my novel, then back at him. Reading appealed to me more than putting pressure on my sore joints—and I knew a walk with Boa would likely lead to some form of studying—but we were nearing the end of our first month in the program. I wanted to be back at baseline by the second, and relaxing in bed wouldn't help me do that.

I set my book down and pushed myself up.

Boa seemed apprehensive about entering Room 4—perhaps because I shared it with Avarium—but he shook off the hesitation and walked in, offering his arm to help lead me out of the quarter.

"You miss the library?" he asked.

"Almost as much as you miss me."

"Oh, *haha*, Evaris."

It took forever to reach the next floor up. The spiral staircase was no easy feat in my current condition, but we got there nonetheless. Surprisingly enough, it felt good to stretch my limbs.

We must have spent an hour or two with the library to ourselves. Boa flipped through guardian memoirs, as usual, while filling me in on what I'd missed over the past few days.

"You're not the only one having a hard time with the latest dose." He started fidgeting with his pencil. "That same day, only half of us showed up to our afternoon classes."

"Yeah, but I must be one of the last to get back on schedule."

He waved his pencil at me. "Just be glad you didn't pass out."

It was quiet for a moment. I found myself curious about Toll and the death threats he'd been receiving—allegedly. Ever since Silver had broken the news to me last week, I hadn't found a private moment with Boa to bring it up. Now that I did, I wasn't sure if I *should*. Perhaps the whole ordeal had blown over by now—Silver hadn't mentioned any new drama when he'd brought supper up to my room yesterday.

Still, I couldn't help but wonder who was really behind those notes, or if they existed at all.

"You seem pretty sharp," Boa said out of the blue. "You should come to class tomorrow. Research and Medical, at least." With a grin, he stood from our table and darted down an aisle.

I had no energy to go after him. "What are you doing back there?"

He reappeared a few seconds later with a chessboard. I recognized its carvings—it was from the lobby outside our quarters.

"Krevall and I brought it up the other day." Boa placed the board between us, followed by two velvet bags of pieces.

"I thought you didn't like the guy," I said.

He shrugged. "I give the Miranda boys a hard time because they think their success is guaranteed. But they're really not that bad, once you get to know them. And I haven't really had anyone to hang out with, since you've been in bed for so long." He started arranging the pieces onto the checkered boxes—white on my side and black on his. "Anyway, you up for a game? Why am I even asking? You're playing a game with me. Okay?"

"You just want to beat me while my brain is still mushy."

Boa smiled. "A win is a win."

I started losing pieces quickly. Though in my defense, he took forever to make his moves. I could have sworn I once waited ten minutes for him to touch a piece—only to let go and keep thinking.

"Chess without me? I'm offended!" someone said. I thought it was Silver at first, but I looked over to see Krevall standing tall in the doorway. "You better let me play the winner."

"That'll be me," Boa said, before our game had even ended.

Krevall was a bit unsteady on his feet as he made his way over. "It's been a while, Starfall." He took the seat next to me. "You back in class?"

I shook my head. The fact that he asked meant he wasn't either.

"Same. Though I can probably get back tomorrow."

"Shh." Boa locked eyes with the board, spinning a pencil in his hand again. "I'm trying to focus."

I rolled my eyes. "You're already winning. Let's just call it."

"No. I need to practice my endgame."

I reached over and knocked down my king.

"Oh, cut it, Evaris!"

"Oh, shut it, Boa! I want to see you play Krevall."

"But I was so close to..." He trailed off, giving in as Krevall started rearranging my white pieces. I scooted my chair aside so he'd have better access to the board.

"You know, this whole poison thing really sucks." Krevall placed his king down with a fury. "What are the odds that a member of the Underground somehow wields your weapon and uses it against you? I mean, immunity can't be *that* helpful, can it? Really, is it worth the trouble?"

"Better safe than sorry," Boa said, rearranging his black pieces.

"Some guardians end up working as taste-testers for the Royal Family," I added. "Tolerance training is extra important for them."

"Ew, yeah. The ones who work in the Palace." Krevall scrunched his nose, making his glasses rise. "They're hardly guardians at all. I need to be in the Defense Division, out in the action, taking down members of the Underground with my bare hands."

"You must read too many hero tales," I replied.

"They're called *guardian memoirs*." Boa laughed like he'd made the funniest joke in the world.

"Right," I said, but I was already checking out of the conversation. Whether I was tracing members of the Underground as a Defense guardian, interrogating them in the Detainment Facility as a Research guardian, or preparing poison and laced tools as a Medical guardian—I couldn't care less. My guardian division didn't matter, so long as I *was* a guardian.

That was all I was focused on right now—the art of becoming.

Krevall pulled a stopwatch out of his pocket. He must've known, from having battled Boa in chess before, that he took too long. They played a faster game than the previous, with moves limited to five minutes—quite generous, in my opinion. I got a kick out of watching Boa's eyes jump from the board to the clock, and then to the board again.

As the game went on, Krevall's pieces pushed forward, crowding Boa's side. It reached a point where he was taking out black pieces almost every move. And when it came to the endgame, Boa put up a good fight, but it wasn't good enough.

Krevall adjusted his glasses and put Boa's king in checkmate.

"I call a rematch," Boa said.

"As you wish."

They played again. Boa lost again.

That was a pattern I noticed the next day, and the day after, as the three of us continued to play chess together at night. Sometimes Silver stretched and watched too, waiting for me to wrap up and join him for training in the courtyard. Chess was a nice way to debrief after the chaos of another day in the program—a chance for us to be kids again, just for an hour or two.

Toll joined only once. He wouldn't stop shaking his foot under the table. "You okay?" I whispered.

He nodded, forced a smile, and volunteered to play against Krevall next. *Check, check, check...*

After getting ready the following morning, murmurs echoed from the common room downstairs. I was the last trainee to join the gathering of boys near the Academy's front door. They were too preoccupied to notice my arrival.

I found my way to Boa and Silver. "What's going on?"

Boa rubbed his temple, and Silver gave me a regretful look. "Remember that thing I told you about?" he whispered.

My blood ran cold. Had Toll seriously killed a horse? I had doubted that he'd follow through with his plan, but perhaps I should have spoken to him just in case.

I looked around, but he wasn't here. Neither was my roommate.

My pulse quickened. "Where are—"

"The guardians are questioning Avarium." Silver's voice was tight. "Oh, Evaris, you should've seen what she did to it. The blood is just—it's—"

"It's really not that bad," Boa assured me. "I've seen dead horses before."

I frowned at Silver. He had claimed that Toll was planning to *frame* Avarium. Why did he assume that she had actually done it?

But I had a more important question to ask first: "What about Toll?"

Silver lowered his head. "He filtered himself this morning."

"*What?*" Clearly he had accomplished his goal of framing Avarium—the guardians were questioning her. Why hadn't he stuck around?

Silver started to pale again. "Let's go outside."

I followed him and Boa through the front door into the summer air. In the distance lay a white horse on the grass, its body sprawled out. I was too far away to make much of what happened.

Silver shut the door and gestured for us to walk with him down the courtyard. We stopped right past the statue of Emperor Vakoi.

"Toll didn't do it," he confessed. "He came at me this morning, all angry, claiming I told everyone about his plan. Which I didn't, of course. But somehow, word got out. Avarium must have caught wind of it and took action first to make a point. He didn't want to risk sticking around to find out what she'd do next. So he left, right after seeing the horse."

I brushed past him, marching toward the white limbs in the distance.

"Hey!" Silver yelled.

I heard Boa running after me. "Wait up!"

Ignoring them both, I trekked onward, biting back my regret. The carcass was already attracting flies.

With my eyes on my black boots, I walked up to the horse, identifying it by the number branded on its shoulder, right under the flower emblem.

My fingers rolled into fists at my sides. This was *my* horse. It was just a day from retirement. *Not that its fate would be any different.*

Its body featured multiple dagger penetrations. But most prominent were the shallow cuts along its torso, which formed a note:

CHIMA

The boy Avarium had killed.
A few drops of blood ran over the letters of his name.

The guardians grilled us, searching for the culprit.
The cooks grilled the horse, because the culprit wasn't found.
Three boys couldn't stomach our punishment.

PART 2
STRATEGY

CHAPTER 8

OPENING

Day 40 | 13 trainees remaining

♫ SILVER JET - ROLLER DERBY ♫

Cal Avarium never mentioned my absence. I certainly gave her the opportunity during my brief stops at Room 4 to shower, change, or grab books from my desk. Sometimes I even sparked a conversation to see if she might finally ask, *Where have you been sleeping, Evaris?*

I wasn't trying to provoke her. I just wanted a human reaction to prove the rumors wrong.

Two weeks ago, when Toll filtered himself, the guardians announced the result of their questioning—they'd found no indication that Avarium had slain the horse. A rumor spread within hours that they were protecting her. *The Force will always take her side*, they said, *just like they've done before, no matter the crime.*

Two trainees filtered themselves after our punishment at supper, fearing what she might get away with next. A third followed, but only once he'd chugged a vial of antiserum. We hadn't been served a dose of belladonna serum—he just wanted the horse meat out of his system before going home.

He wouldn't take any piece of the Academy with him.

Since then, we'd traveled in company and never turned our backs, even on those we trusted. I once invited Boa to train with Silver and me, only to find that Silver had invited Nash.

We didn't fully believe Avarium had done it. All we knew was that it wasn't Toll.

The real culprit could still be among us.

Worst of all, that dream came back. I spent every night browsing my uncle's fabric shop, hearing a background hum of dread. When he'd joke with me, that pit in my stomach would shrink. And just as I'd let my guard down, he'd wrap his arms around me and squeeze, squeeze, squeeze—until his face morphed into Avarium's.

I would burst up, gasping, and look over at my roommate's bed. Sometimes she was there; sometimes she wasn't.

I wondered where she was when she wasn't.

Frankly, it was too much wondering to handle. So every night, after training with Silver in the courtyard, I'd shower and head back to the library. Boa and Krevall were often still playing chess. After a few extra games, I'd study off to the side alone—or with Nash if he was there too. Sometimes he waited for Krevall to wrap up. They were roommates, and I didn't blame him for not wanting to be in their quarter alone at this hour.

Once everyone started blinking faster and yawning, I'd tell them, *Get some rest. I'm gonna read a bit longer.* And they'd shoot me a concerned look on their way out that faded more with each passing day.

Tonight, it faded completely, because they didn't give me a look at all. They simply left.

When their footsteps faded, I closed my history book and rested my head in my arms. The same vivid images came back, despite how hard I tried to fend them off.

I saw my white horse, dead in the field.

Bloody cuts spelling the name of a boy my age.

Avarium, staring at me with her hollow eyes.

Over the next month, we carried on almost like ordinary students. The horse-slayer didn't strike again, and we didn't face a single filtration. We simply attended classes, studied, and drank our beet juice—my post-dose symptoms lately made me miss one day instead of three. I was starting to build a tolerance.

With so much time having passed, most of us had concluded that the horse-slayer was one of the three boys who had filtered themselves after our punishment. Perhaps our instructors' intense reaction had scared him off —made him realize that he'd taken his sabotage too far and couldn't afford to get caught.

Once we accepted this theory, we weren't so afraid to be alone anymore. I'd gone back to sleeping in Room 4 a couple of weeks ago, though I still spent my early nights in the library playing chess before training with Silver. I preferred heading to bed long after Avarium had fallen asleep.

But the relief could only last for so long. Commander Roz finally announced our long-awaited filtration: "Tomorrow, you'll each face a sparring partner. The trainee who loses their match the fastest will go home."

I headed to the library as usual that night, despite the urge to train twice as long instead. I knew it would only make me more exhausted tomorrow. Resting my body counted as preparation too.

As I neared the third floor, a strange tapping noise from above caught my attention. I headed farther upstairs to investigate, but when I reached the fourth floor, the noise still echoed overhead. It was coming from the fifth. I didn't know anyone who spent this hour up there. All it had was the Medical lab, the infirmary, and a few supply closets.

I made my way to the highest floor and stepped off the landing into the dim hallway. Someone had left the lab door open, and that same clinking sound came from within. I crept forward and peered into the room. Moonlight shone through the curved, glass-paneled walls and ceiling, illuminating a sole trainee behind one of the standing lab desks. In one hand, he held a single boot, and in the other, a hammer. He kept hitting the boot's sole.

My blood ran cold. *Krevall.*

According to Commander Roz, our boots had weights in them. It would make the final five faster after graduation, once we transitioned into lighter guardian boots, he'd explained. I hadn't fully believed him; his boots looked heavier than ours. This skepticism had led me to remove the insole from my boot and press at the leather underneath. I felt something hard, like metal. The weights were probably real, but I couldn't verify without taking tools to my boot.

Which Krevall was doing right in front of me. Was he trying to give himself an advantage? Without weights, he'd be lighter on his feet than the rest of us during our filtration.

I slipped through the partially open door, my lips downturned. "So you're a cobbler now?"

Krevall flinched, nearly dropping his boot and hammer.

I walked over, arms crossed, and he looked up with wide eyes.

"Oh, it's you." He sighed in relief. "Caught me red-handed."

Red-handed?

I stopped on the opposite side of his desk, forcing a stern expression as my heart skipped a beat. Had he just confessed to more than the one offense I'd caught him for? If he was playing dirty for tomorrow, what if he had done so in the past? Could he have been the uniform-cutter, the flower-giver, and the horse-slayer?

"I come from a family of cobblers." He observed the black boot in his hand. "Their work doesn't do much for the Vakoi Empire, but it's... humble."

I held my expression, unsure whether to believe him.

Krevall tilted his head. The moment he recognized my assumption, he burst into laughter.

"Relax! I got a nail in my shoe." He rotated the boot so I could see the nail pierced through his sole at an angle. "I'm not trying to get the weights out. Trust me, Nash tried that last month, and now he's got a hole in his. He's too scared to ask the guardians for a replacement."

I exhaled, my heart settling. "Can't you just pull it out?"

"No way. It's really jammed in there. I can't even get it with the claw."

"So now you're burying it deeper?"

"Well, what else am I supposed to do? At least I won't feel it that way."

I concealed a grin. Perhaps Krevall's chess-minded brain kept him from seeing the simplest solution.

"Let me have that," I said, reaching for the boot.

His hands gave up easily, but his mouth put up a fight. "Trust me. Anything you try, I've already..."

He trailed off. The nail was nearly out already. All I'd done was drag the sole against the desk until the head caught the edge. From there, it only took a bit of force at an angle for the nail to budge.

"It's like using a thimble to push a needle instead of your finger." I pinched the nail and pulled it cleanly out of his boot. "If you're not strong enough, use something stronger. Hence, this table."

"Well, would you look at that?" Krevall smiled at the hole left behind. After a moment, his eyes darted to me. "I like how you think, Starfall."

My cheeks warmed. It was the first time my last name didn't feel like an embarrassment.

"You know," he continued, "there's something I've been meaning to ask you."

"Go on."

Krevall stared at the hammer in his grip. "What exactly are you trying to prove to your family?"

I shrugged and set his boot on the desk between us. "That I can do something great without them."

He narrowed his eyes, as though he were testing me. "If you don't want to work in fashion, there are other career paths aside from guardianship. It's not one or the other."

"For me it is," I countered. "My parents won't financially support anything outside of what they approve of. Guardianship is all I can accomplish on my own."

"You could get a trade apprenticeship. Plenty are free, or even paid."

"Just to land an obscure job in the end? That would prove nothing to the Starfalls. Guardians, however—well, they respect them."

"There it is." Krevall pointed his hammer at me. "I knew it!"

I leaned back a little. "Huh?"

"I had a feeling we were the same." He smiled and took his boot back. "My family runs a well-known shop in Miranda. They always expected me to take it over someday. And if not that, what were my other options? Working at a market, or a Saver Store, or in some trade like farming or textiles? There's just nothing that warms the heart quite like taking down people who do us real harm."

I forced a smile, only because he seemed excited. Our motivations didn't truly align like he thought. Beyond proving my family wrong, I saw no appeal in the grandiosity of guardianship.

But maybe I could learn something from his perspective. Maybe my opportunity at the Academy could be more than an escape from my family's expectations. Maybe it could also be a chance to take part in something bigger than myself.

For the first time, I felt a different kind of pride while imagining my success in the program. I could make a real difference in taking down the Underground, the same monsters who had gouged out eyes, among other heinous crimes. Maybe that mission could be my real spark.

Krevall and I faced the door as footsteps echoed outside the lab.

"There you are!" It was Boa. "Come on, I've been waiting downstairs."

"You two go ahead." Krevall leaned toward me. "I've gotta put these tools away first."

I nodded and joined Boa in the hallway, passing on the word. "He'll be right down. You'll have to put up with my game in the meantime."

Boa smiled. "Nothing wrong with an easy warm-up."

<hr>

"Single file!"

We scattered into place in front of Commander Roz, as we did every afternoon, but my body sure knew it wasn't any other day. I couldn't stop shaking. It felt like forever since our last filtration.

Commander Roz walked down our line, studying us, pretending to plan whom to pair up with whom. I was certain he already knew what to test in each trainee and exactly whom to pair them with to test it.

As he passed me, our eyes locked, and I reminded myself that I didn't need to win today. He would time our matches, pair by pair. I could lose

—that was fine—but I couldn't lose the fastest. I needed to put up a strong fight. *Simple. That's all I need to do.*

Which was a *hard* thing to do, I corrected, since everyone else was aiming to do the same thing.

"Starfall and Avarium," Commander Roz said.

To my left and right, Boa and Silver sighed in relief, but I could count several boys I'd rather spar against instead of my roommate.

I looked over to spot Avarium farther down our single-file line. She didn't meet my gaze.

Commander Roz announced the next pairings, but I tuned him out, biting back the injustice. To the boys, it might have looked like our instructor showed mercy by pairing me against the only other girl—but I had studied her enough to know that she was always one step ahead, with faster strikes and harder blows. And I wouldn't even have the privilege of half speed, half power this time around.

Commander Roz and I both knew that Avarium was the better fighter. I had seen how he watched her. Perhaps he wanted me to lose this match because he saw promise in her and wanted her to win. Did he plan for me to be his tool today?

Like hell. I rolled my hands into fists at my sides.

Since Commander Roz had announced our pairing first, we were to spar first. Avarium and I squared up in the middle of the training room on what we called the green zone. This circular area of about ten steps in diameter was emerald instead of black. If one of us stepped or fell outside of its bounds, it'd be an instant loss.

The boys gathered around the green zone as I raised my hands, mirroring Avarium.

Commander Roz clicked a button on his golden stopwatch. "Begin."

She came at me like thunder. Loud, hard, and so fast I could only hear and not see her. I stumbled back, my boot nearly sliding off the green zone.

Without a moment to spare, she threw a punch. I ducked and rose with a shove that had no real grace but all the strength I could muster.

Some boy snickered, but I brushed my embarrassment aside. I couldn't distract myself with how I might look to everyone else. I just needed to last as long as possible. Hell, if I focused, maybe I could even win.

Avarium recovered without breaking a sweat, and her hollow eyes made me think of my white horse, dead in the field, bloody cuts spelling the name of a boy my age.

While I wasn't convinced she was to blame, I chose to believe—if only for the duration of this match—that she had done *everything*. Avarium was the uniform-cutter, the flower-giver, the horse-slayer...

I didn't bother kicking because I knew how fast she was. A single catch could ruin me. Instead, I shot forward with a string of consecutive strikes. One punch was bound to land eventually, and she would stumble right back into the—

I gasped for air.

Avarium had blocked a punch and countered with a fist to my gut. The force knocked the air out of me so fast that the world seemed to turn quiet, fully quiet.

My lungs constricted until I choked.

Through my fading vision, Avarium's fist flashed ahead of me. It collided with my jawline and sent a numbing shock through my entire skull.

I failed to break my fall.

As my head struck the floor, the world exploded with noise again. Boys winced and called my name, but the pain paralyzed me.

A pair of ironclad hands gripped my arms and lifted me slightly off the floor. I couldn't struggle back as they dragged me off the green zone.

Commander Roz's stopwatch was no longer ticking.

"Forty-three seconds," he announced.

My vision faded completely.

Doctor Blimmery held a lantern up to study my eyes' reaction to the light. No brain damage—to his dismay, I was sure.

"Forty-three seconds," he said. "That's a quick loss."

"Not quick enough to go home." I couldn't help but boast a little. I was the second-fastest to lose, which meant I had barely scraped by. Well, scraping by was enough for me. Scraping by was enough to win, if I played my cards right.

Doctor Blimmery shook his head and pulled the lantern away. "It's not too late to leave, you know. But once you make the final five, retirement is the only way out."

"I'm aware."

"And you won't be able to get married, or have any relationship of a similar nature."

"I know what I signed up for, Doctor."

He stared blankly, unblinking. "Not everyone in the Force is good, Ev."

I squinted. Of course they were. They were *guardians*. It was one of the most respected jobs in the Empire. Perhaps he was implying that difficult personalities existed in the Force, which was to be expected from a program this competitive. Why would he think I was too delicate to deal with people like that?

Doctor Blimmery changed the subject, his tone suddenly upbeat. "Well, you're lucky it's only a light concussion. A few days off will do you well." He stood and offered a hand to help me downstairs. I took it only because I'd never had a concussion before. I couldn't risk falling and obtaining additional injuries.

We parted ways once he brought me to the second-floor lobby. I was about to head to my room when I spotted Krevall slumped over on a sofa, eyes on the floor. He had a black eye and some bruises on his arms—shown off prominently by how he'd rolled up his sleeves.

"Ouch." I made my way toward him, cautious on my feet. "Who turned you blue?"

He offered a subtle smile. Something about him looked different, but I couldn't put my finger on it.

I sat next to him. "Did you win at least?"

"Barely."

"Well, congratulations."

He chuckled. "And congratulations to you, *second-best loser*."

I didn't laugh. It wasn't as empowering when it came from someone else.

"Sorry," he muttered.

"No, I mean, it's true, after all."

Krevall hesitated. "If it makes you feel any better, at least you don't have to deal with *this*." He picked up his glasses and turned them over in his hands. Cracks cut through the lenses like spiderwebs. That's why he looked different—he wasn't wearing them.

"How bad are your eyes?"

"I wouldn't wear glasses to Defense class if I didn't *really* needed to." He leaned in close to my face. "Let's just say I can barely see you right now."

I flinched when his hands brushed my ears, sliding his glasses to rest on my nose. Instantly, there were two of him, bright streaks of light cutting through the twin Krevalls. Everything else warped and slipped in and out of focus. I ripped the glasses off in fear of the eye strain impacting my concussion.

He took them back gingerly, as though they were still valuable. Then he remembered they were broken and flung them aside on the sofa.

"Maybe you can get new ones," I said.

"If the guardians didn't replace Gup's uniforms, why replace my glasses?" He chuckled bitterly. "Why cater to my condition when someone perfectly healthy could fill my place?"

"It doesn't mean you're unhealthy, Krevall. So what if you can't see as well? You just need to work harder from now on. Hold the books up closer. Whatever you have to do."

He stared ahead, nodding a bit, but I was certain my words hadn't cheered him up.

I sighed. We had both shown weakness today. There were only twelve of us now, and more than half would still go home. I was certain the other trainees already saw me as one of the next to go—and without his glasses, perhaps Krevall had slipped a little in their estimation too.

He cleared his throat, breaking our silence. "I don't know if this means anything, but I'm glad you're still here, Starfall."

The air rushed out of me for the second time that day when he placed a hand on mine.

I nearly shook it off and scolded him for being careless—but a pair of footsteps from the staircase spooked him for me. He yanked his hand away just as another trainee stepped off the landing.

Boa shuffled to a stop and frowned. "What are you doing?"

"Nothing," I blurted.

Krevall kicked his feet up on the low table in front of us. "Just hanging out, Boa. Big milestone today." He leaned back on the cushions.

"Oh. Okay." Boa's voice came out stiff. He glanced at me before rushing into his room, his steps abnormally loud.

My cheeks burned. Did Boa really believe I'd be foolish enough to make a romantic advance on a fellow trainee? Perhaps I wasn't the most dedicated person here, but I had standards. I wasn't the type to distract myself with romance, especially in a program like this.

"I'm gonna take a nap," I whispered.

"Yeah, you get some rest," Krevall said. "You hit your head pretty hard there."

I approached Room 4 and looked back one last time.

Krevall smiled and waved, his expression apologetic.

My eyes widened. His feet were propped up on the table, and I could see his soles. There was no hole where that nail used to be.

He hadn't been tinkering with his own boot that night.

CHAPTER 9

GAMBIT

Day 75 | 12 trainees remaining

♫ HUNTER · PARIS PALOMA ♫

Cal Avarium was always watching. I just didn't know it yet.

Three days had passed since our sparring filtration. Due to my concussion, I couldn't attend classes—Doctor Blimmery said I needed to give my mind and body a break. I only interacted with my fellow trainees during meals and recreation time. That's when I trailed behind them as they walked, eyes low, waiting to glimpse their soles.

I was looking for a hole I never found.

Every boot was perfect, including Nash's, despite Krevall's claim that his roommate had tampered with them and was too scared to ask the guardians for a replacement.

Today was my first day back in class after my concussion, and Commander Roz paired me with the same girl who had caused it. While Avarium and I ran drills, I kept looking at Krevall, studying his boots the next time he kicked, just to be sure. Had coming from a family of cobblers given him the experience needed to patch his sole up so seamlessly that I couldn't even notice the correction?

Then came my darker theory. Maybe Krevall *hadn't* come from a family of cobblers—and that lie, along with the nail he'd purposely planted in someone else's boot, had served as a cover-up so I wouldn't notice what he was actually up to in the lab that night.

Punch, block, redirect.

My turn. Block, punch, punch.

We went back and forth, repeating the pattern. There were several times I raised the wrong hand or stepped in the incorrect direction to dodge. Avarium repeatedly had to stop and reset.

Commander Roz looped by. "Is there a problem, Starfall?"

I shook my head. He marched to his next victim.

Once we were back in sync, Avarium started making odd sounds. I thought she was winded at first, but I soon realized that she was whispering.

"I"—another block—"know"—a punch—"about"—she redirected my attack—"Krevall."

My eyes widened, and I fell out of rhythm again. We reset.

"Keep up," Avarium warned.

"I am," I snapped.

We started over, and she continued speaking between breaths. "Krevall did something to the filtered trainee's boot. Made him awkward on his feet. That's why he fell out of the green zone so quickly."

I narrowed my eyes. If the filtered boy had lost due to a defective boot, he would have worn the evidence of Krevall's sabotage home. That would explain why no one here had a hole.

Still, I shook the idea away. If Avarium was right, that meant *I* might have been the first-place loser, not the second, had everyone played fair.

"That can't be true," I whispered, throwing a punch.

"You just don't want to believe it."

I started to look in Krevall's direction, but Avarium sent an unexpected punch my way, forcing me to block her instead.

"That wasn't in the drill," I said.

She frowned.

"Next!" Commander Roz yelled.

We split into new pairs. Boa offered a smile as we got into position. We hardly worked together in Defense class, but I wasn't able to return the gesture.

As we practiced a new drill, I kept thinking about Avarium. She was meticulous. Focused. Always on time. Perhaps I'd be a fool *not* to believe her.

The following day, after Research class, the bell called us to Medical. Krevall usually headed there with his roommate Nash, but he had asked Professor Embre to use the restroom a few minutes prior. She had probably only said yes because he'd been brushing her ego all morning by asking hollow questions and calling her antidotes clever.

"And in one of the memoirs, the guardian said that—"

"Hold that thought, Boa." I was already rushing for the door. "I gotta grab something before Medical!"

There were a few other boys in the hallway already. I swerved around them and was first to the staircase, racing up toward the fifth floor. *He must be up to something.*

Krevall had only bought himself a few minutes. With such little time, he couldn't sneak around without showing up late to our next class. That is, unless he was sneaking around in the same room where our next class would take place. Three minutes could be valuable in that case.

Heel to toe...

As I neared the landing, I slowed my steps.

Bend your knees...

The door to the lab was open, and I heard footsteps from within. I pressed myself against the wall by the door and peered inside.

Krevall stood at Avarium's standing lab desk with a handful of brown beans in his gloved hand—belladonna's antidote. We had worked with calabar beans during Medical class before. Against belladonna, it served as an emergency neutralizer. On its own, it was just as poisonous.

Krevall slipped the beans into Avarium's gloves. They could easily give her rashes.

His eyes shot to the door, and I whipped my head away. A few seconds passed. Then I heard footsteps. I peered back in.

Krevall stood at his usual desk, reviewing his Medical notebook as if he'd simply shown up early. If he was capable of this, maybe Avarium was right about him having messed with the filtered trainee's boot. And if he had done that, who was to say he wasn't behind the other acts too?

My cheeks flushed. I had spent weeks playing chess with Krevall every night. I had even comforted him when his glasses broke—and in response, he had placed his hand on mine. What if that whole conversation was a distraction from his odd behavior the night before? Maybe he knew he'd blundered by mentioning a hole in Nash's boot and claiming he needed to put away *tools* when he only had a single hammer out.

But why was he trying to give Avarium rashes? It seemed like a petty form of sabotage until I remembered how everyone had calmed down since the horse killing. Most of us assumed the culprit was one of the boys who had gone home that same day. Now Krevall wanted to send a message that the saboteur was still among us—that we had never been safe and still weren't.

Paranoia was about to spread like wildfire.

I have to warn Avarium.

I stepped toward the staircase a bit too loudly.

"Oh, hey, Starfall."

I stopped, fully visible from the doorway, and made eye contact with Krevall. He smiled and waved as though I hadn't caught him. He likely assumed that I'd just gotten here.

A chill ran down my spine. Now we both needed to play dumb.

"Hey." I forced a smile and joined him in the lab, taking my usual spot.

As more trainees trickled in, I pulled my crinkled Medical notes out of my book bag and scattered the pages across my desk. Nash joined Krevall; Boa joined me.

"Evaris, these are your notes?" Boa lifted my papers gingerly, as if he might hurt them. "How do you even find what you need?"

I stared at Krevall as he laughed at something Nash said.

"Hey." Boa nudged my shoulder, snapping me out of my daze. "Why are you staring at Krevall?"

I frowned. "I'm not."

"You've been staring at him a lot lately."

The door opened behind us, and we looked over in unison as Doctor Blimmery wheeled a metal cart into the room. It contained twelve wooden boxes, one for each of us.

Boa's eyes lit up, instantly forgetting our previous topic of discussion. He grabbed my arm and whispered, "It's the rabbit filtration. I've read about this."

My heart skipped a beat. "*Filtration*?"

Doctor Blimmery made his way down the aisle, sliding a box in front of each of us. Boa stood up straight, starry-eyed, as the rest of us looked around in confusion.

"In today's filtration, we'll be testing your restraint." Doctor Blimmery reached his own desk at the end of the room and faced us, clasping his hands together. "Boxes open!"

Boa opened his box and marveled at its contents.

I opened mine to find a rabbit inside.

Well, a rabbit—and a dagger.

"You kids know the drill. If you fail this test, we send you home." Doctor Blimmery clicked a button on his golden stopwatch, and its ticking noise filled the lab. "You have five minutes to kill a rabbit."

No one wanted to do it bare-handed. I reached for my gloves, freezing as I remembered the calabar beans in Avarium's. My roommate stood at the desk right in front of me. I could whisper a warning, but at the very least, that would attract Boa's attention, and he would question me later. Would he even believe me if I were to tell him the truth about Krevall?

Avarium put her gloves on before I could decide what to do. She yanked her hands out almost instantly.

Krevall glanced over, his lips twitching, holding back a grin.

She shook her gloves, and the beans bounced on the table, stealing everyone's attention.

"Is something wrong?" Doctor Blimmery called from across the room.

Avarium stretched her fingers out. A red haze spread across them—the start of nasty rashes.

Mutters erupted. The room grew cold, a familiar paranoia spreading between us.

The horse-slayer had never left.

Krevall gasped and whispered with Nash as though he knew nothing.

Doctor Blimmery crept closer, studying the calabar beans scattered on the floor around Avarium's desk. "Who is responsible for this?"

I scowled ahead, resisting the urge to look in Krevall's direction. His silence made my blood boil, but so did my own. I could have said something to stop Avarium. I *should* have stopped Avarium.

Doctor Blimmery glanced at his stopwatch with a sigh, knowing the culprit wouldn't step forward. "Everyone, back to it!"

In unison, we all remembered that we were being timed.

Avarium reached into her box and pulled out a rabbit. It trembled and drooled as she laid it on her lab table. The guardians had likely injected the poor creature with belladonna so it'd be easier to kill. She gripped the dagger with both red hands and pierced the rabbit's heart.

She was the first to kill. And she did it without gloves.

I gulped hard.

"Wash your hands," Doctor Blimmery ordered.

A trace of blood marked the doorknob on her way out.

Next to me, Boa plopped his rabbit onto our desk. I slipped my gloves on and rushed to pull mine out next. There was something cruel about how limp it was, all drugged up like this. And as I'd struggled to pour worms into boiling water, I couldn't seem to push my blade into the rabbit's head.

The sound of squelching flesh made my teeth clench. Boa had finished the task. He didn't seem conflicted as Doctor Blimmery dismissed him.

Silver looked away as he raised his blade, lips pursed. He hated blood, but I was certain he'd find the strength to handle this. Just as I would.

With my eyes closed, I did the job. The sound of my rabbit's death coated my tongue in a bitter taste. Even through my thick gloves, I felt the warmth of its blood.

"Thank you, Ev. You're dismissed."

I ripped off my gloves and left them on the desk, not sparing the carcass a glance. With steady steps, I exited the lab, already knowing the blood on the doorknob had stained my hands too.

Once in the hallway, I ran straight to the infirmary. The taste in my mouth thickened until I gagged.

My breakfast came up in the infirmary sink, joining the blood Avarium had washed off. I didn't even bother to clean my hands. I was disgusting all around. I needed a shower. I needed to apologize to Avarium.

"Hey."

I looked over to see my roommate sitting on an infirmary bed with a jar of salve.

"I've known guys like him." Avarium rubbed the yellow cream over her hands, turning her blisters shiny. "If you ignore them, they get worse."

I gripped the sink to keep myself upright. Was she referring to Chima?

She raised her chin to meet my gaze. "Krevall needs to go."

After field class, I sat in the library with Boa, Silver, Krevall, and Nash. The filtration had resulted in one trainee going home for failing to kill his rabbit, but no one was talking about him. Instead, we discussed the mystery of the saboteur's return—though I barely spoke in fear of rage dripping into my voice. It took all I had not to scowl or chuckle at Krevall's faked innocence.

"Maybe Avarium put the beans in her own gloves," Nash considered. "It would line up with giving herself those flowers."

"I don't know." Krevall frowned at the table, deep in thought. "I got some calabar rashes last month, remember? They're *awful*. Giving herself flowers is one thing, but I doubt she'd purposely suffer."

I could've slapped him in the face.

"She's killed a boy," Boa argued. "What *wouldn't* she do?"

"And she hardly reacted to the beans in her gloves." Silver nodded to himself. "It's like they hardly surprised her."

The three innocents among the four would never solve this, would they? Especially if they always included Krevall in the discussion. He could sway them in the wrong directions, and they'd trust him every time.

"I'm gonna take a nap," I blurted out, not knowing what a better excuse might be.

They exchanged glances. Krevall looked confused, but I couldn't trust the emotions on his face anymore. I could only hope that he didn't know I was onto him.

"See you later," I added, offering a quick wave. I didn't hear them resume their discussion as I left the library—they were watching me. The last thing I needed was to draw unnecessary attention to myself, so I'd have to conjure a cover-up for my odd behavior later.

I looped down the spiral staircase, reaching the common room on the first floor in record time. I knocked on the door to the guardian quarters and waited.

No response.

I knocked again.

Soon enough, footsteps sounded on the other side, and Doctor Blimmery greeted me. Perhaps my expression concerned him—before I could speak, he headed for the Academy's front door, gesturing for me to follow. "Let's take a walk, shall we?"

We ventured onto the Academy field, and I shivered as a breeze washed over us. It was nearing the end of summer, so the weather was cooling down, especially in the evenings.

"Talk to me," Doctor Blimmery said. It was an invitation, not an order.

"Krevall killed the horse," I replied, matter-of-factly. I was about to share how I'd seen him tinkering with a boot on the night before our recent sparring filtration—but then I forced my lips together. Technically, if Krevall hadn't sabotaged his boot, I might have been the trainee who deserved to go home that day. I couldn't risk Doctor Blimmery retroactively filtering me.

So I explained today's incident alone: "I saw Krevall put calabar beans in Avarium's gloves."

Doctor Blimmery's eyes wandered afar. "That proves nothing about the horse."

"Of course it does. He's the only person who's been caught performing an act of sabotage. It's pattern recognition."

"To start, do you have any evidence about the beans?"

"No, but—"

His heavy sigh cut me off. "If pointed fingers could send trainees home, then any of you could lie and pull the program into chaos. What we want is a confession."

"So you won't even look into it? I need to launch an investigation myself and gather indisputable evidence?"

"I believe you, Ev."

"*Huh?*"

"Listen closely." Doctor Blimmery leaned toward me as we walked. "It is my goal, with selecting trainees, to vouch for the kindest kids, because the Force needs more of them. But the other two look for the most rugged kids, who tend to cause more trouble. And thus, there are bullies with every cycle, though some are worse than others. You can imagine it doesn't fare well when I tell my fellow instructors that it's *their* picks who cause the problems, even if that's how the story always goes. Without evidence, my efforts toward a fairer program look like favoritism of *my* choices and criticism of *theirs*. Do you see what I mean?"

I did see what he meant, but I didn't like it.

"I cannot incite punishments based on instinct alone," he continued. "I cannot afford to further exhaust their trust in my judgment."

I looked away with a scoff. This was a grand excuse, wasn't it? "You just don't like that *I'm* the one to come forward. If anyone else reported their suspicions of Krevall, you'd at least entertain the idea."

Doctor Blimmery knew exactly what I was getting at. "I may have spoken against your selection, Ev, but now that you're here, I can't get in your way."

"How do I know for sure? Who's to say you have no control over my success in the program, as one of the Academy guardians yourself?"

His lips curled in disgust. "If I can't send Krevall home without a verified cause, the same applies to you. It doesn't matter how I feel about your presence here."

"And how *do* you feel about me, Doctor?"

"I think you are prideful," he said with a single nod, "and there is more than enough pride in the Force."

My eyes burned.

If the guardians won't help me, I'll have to do this on my own.

CHAPTER 10

FORK

Day 75 | 11 trainees remaining

♫ TWO MINDS - AMELIA MAGDALENA ♫

Cal Avarium was not the forgiving type. I could tell by the look in her eyes when she told me Krevall needed to go.

Naturally, I avoided conversation that night. I hadn't played chess or trained with Silver to avoid any chance of running into Krevall. I couldn't deal with being around him any longer today. So instead, I locked myself in Room 4 much earlier than usual.

Avarium was still awake, sitting at her desk, struggling to study. She'd snuck a container of salve from the infirmary, from which she kept reapplying cream when she caught herself scratching. Sometimes she smacked her hands to suppress the unbearable itch.

I pretended to read in bed, mentally crafting an apology—or excuses to avoid it. Finally, though, I swallowed my embarrassment.

"Sorry." I was hardly audible.

Avarium rubbed more salve onto her rashes. "You didn't do it."

"But I saw him do it, and I didn't tell you."

She sat sideways in her seat to make eye contact. "I wouldn't expect you to. Considering how the boys treat Gup."

I put my book down. Most boys still kept their distance from Gup outside of class, even after he and Avarium stopped eating together. His brief friendship with her lingered in their minds. If I'd helped her, the others might have looked at me the same way. The fact that she knew this made me feel even worse. If only she'd assumed the rabbit filtration had simply distracted me.

Avarium walked over and sat on the end of my bed. I could tell she was about to steer the conversation to Krevall—it would be too risky to speak about him from opposite sides of the room. Our walls were so thin that we'd often hear footsteps and running water from the adjacent boys' living quarters.

"You're the only other person who suspects him," Avarium said in a hushed voice. "That's why I'm trusting you with this information. But it needs to stay between us."

"Of course." I sat up straighter against the pillows behind me.

"Do you remember the first boy who went home, because he scored the lowest on our assignment?"

I nodded.

"That was Krevall's doing too," she finished.

"But Professor Embre left class with our papers. He couldn't have accessed them."

"He knew how to pick locks long before we learned in field class." She leaned toward me. "I saw him grab metal scraps from our tool crafting equipment in the lab. He used them to open the door to the guardian quarters when they weren't there. And he had a pencil in his back pocket, which I'm sure he used to swap the names on his paper with the filtered trainee's."

"So you think he turned in a bad essay and claimed the other boy's work as his own?" I whispered.

"I'm certain."

"Why? One trainee would get sent home anyway."

"Commander Roz used to compliment the boy he sabotaged. Krevall considered him a threat."

I looked at the lantern on Avarium's desk, filled with dead flowers, and another piece fell into place. That bouquet had shown up the day after Professor Embre congratulated Gup for scoring highest on our assignment. Commander Roz had also paired Avarium with Gup for dagger training, and they'd proven to be an excellent duo. Perhaps Krevall didn't want two well-performing outcasts banding together.

"He gave you the flowers too, didn't he?"

"I assume," she replied. "But I'm certain he's behind the horse. I followed him out that night."

I frowned. "You caught him *twice*, and he never noticed you?"

"He's not overly careful. People just don't look too hard, because they like him. That's how it always goes. Powerful people don't have to hide their tricks. Everyone's too blind to notice, and if they do, they don't believe it."

I thought of the horse Krevall had killed. *My* horse. He really was the reason I'd spent two weeks sleeping in the library. My stomach twisted at the thought of all the hours I'd wasted with him, losing game after game. *No more.* Chess was one thing, but I wouldn't let him beat me in the program. He deserved to go home.

"I say we strike during the next belladonna dose," Avarium continued. "You weren't there because of your concussion, but he took to the last one pretty hard. Even drank the antiserum to make himself vomit. There's a good chance he'll take it again next time."

I tilted my head. "What are you suggesting?"

"Let's add belladonna to the antiserum vials in the dining hall. Doctor Blimmery doesn't swap them out—they're always under the serving table. We can add the serum tonight and leave them planted for whenever the next dose happens."

"You want to *poison* him?"

"He killed the horse."

"We're talking about a human, not an animal."

"The antiserum contains mustard seed and vinegar to induce vomiting. It's a strong flavor profile, and due to the dose, he won't be in his right mind anyway. I doubt he'll notice the taste of serum where it shouldn't be. He'll pass out instead of vomiting, forcing him to get transferred for an injection of emergency neutralizer."

"That could kill him," I said, raising my voice. "What if he dies before he makes it to Vakoi City Hospital?"

"Shh!" she scolded. "Relax. I'll do the math just right. It won't be enough to hurt him."

"You don't know that."

"We can't let him win."

"Let's just..." I took a deep breath, calming my nerves. "Let's take a step back, okay? We don't need to resort to poison. It's too risky."

For the first time, Avarium's face broke into real, visceral emotion. She looked at me as though I'd stabbed her in the back. Perhaps it took more bravery than I thought for her to trust me with this information.

I softened my voice. "We're just waiting for the right time, okay? We'll do *something*, but not that."

"Okay, Evaris," Avarium replied sharply.

She left my bed and continued studying, scratching her arm with a rage worse than earlier.

I had an extra hard time falling asleep that night.

The next morning welcomed us with a dead rabbit.

Its bloody carcass lay outside Room 7, just as the dead flowers had awaited Avarium.

Silver gagged at the sight. Boa sketched a drawing *for his records*—I had a feeling he was working on a potential guardian memoir of his own.

"Who would do this?" Gup asked, more to himself than anyone else.

I resisted the urge to look at Krevall. The boy who had bruised him and broken his glasses lived in Room 7. This attack was personal.

Would it be a dead trainee who we'd find lying around next?

Finally, the door to Room 7 opened.

The trainee stared at the rabbit in complete and utter horror. He filtered himself within the hour.

Only ten of us remained.

I nearly knocked all the chess pieces off the board as I played a game against Krevall that evening. If he intended to pursue justice as a guardian—and fight against the Underground as part of a united front—how could he sabotage his fellow trainees? Didn't he see the irony?

And where had he found that dead rabbit, anyway? Had he dug it up from wherever the guardians had discarded them? The thought made me *sick*.

"Hey." Krevall interrupted me as I plotted my next move. Boa had just stepped out to use the restroom, briefly leaving us alone. "You seem down."

I forced a fake chuckle and moved a random pawn, giving up on finding the best strategy. "I just had a concussion. Cut me some slack."

Krevall laced his fingers together and stared at the board. "I've been having a tough time too. You know, you missed a dose a couple days ago. It was a rough one. I kept tripping over my feet in Defense class." He moved a pawn in front of mine. "No matter what we do, there's no getting ahead in the program. It's always just one step forward."

"Right." I moved another pawn without thinking, and Krevall captured a rook with his jumping knight. I hadn't even seen it hiding there behind a row of pieces, waiting to strike.

My blood simmered. I captured his rook with my other pawn. *Take that.*

With no time to spare, his queen swooped in and put me in checkmate. Many pieces remained on the board, but my king had nowhere to run. The game was over, just like that.

I looked up with wide eyes, fearing that he'd seen through me—that he finally knew I was onto him.

But what he *thought* had been bothering me was entirely incorrect.

"It didn't mean anything." His voice was quieter now. "When I... touched your hand, okay?"

I gulped, relieved that he'd misread me.

"I know," I replied. "It never happened."

As always, beet juice was served with lunch.

But for the second time, it contained belladonna.

"It's poisoned," I declared after my first sip. I'd become quite good at testing for its slightly sweet flavor. Perhaps because my parents used to pour me glasses of wine while discussing *notes* and *undertones*.

"Couldn't they have waited another week or two?" I added. First, a sparring filtration, then a rabbit-killing filtration, and now *this*? Another belladonna dose, the day after Krevall's targeted trainee had filtered himself?

"Just drink up!" Silver said, which was easy for *him* to say. He and Boa were lucky; they'd usually get tremors and headaches for a few hours at most. Meanwhile, I'd be nauseous and bedridden, with blurry vision that'd earn me extra scolds from Commander Roz upon my return to class.

It was a nasty poison. Doctor Blimmery told us that a paper with traces of belladonna on its edges could kill someone via a poisonous paper cut. *Imagine dying from a paper cut.*

Silver tilted his head back and downed a few gigantic gulps. That big mouth of his helped him complete his dose quickly. His glass was empty before I took my second sip.

"All done," he announced.

I expected to exchange an annoyed look with Boa, but he was staring at his half-empty glass, his hands shaking a little. I figured it must have been a bad dose if he was already showing minor symptoms.

Great. Last week, I had almost taken the antiserum during a dose that Boa and Silver hadn't reacted to. *This will be a bad one.*

On the bright side, I could use my time in bed to think up an alternative plan to get rid of Krevall. I raised my glass and took a longer sip.

I swore I could feel my cheeks redden. I had a severe case of *beet face*, as Boa called it.

"Evaris?"

When I looked up at Boa, my vision lagged.

"Are you okay?" he asked.

"For the glory of Vakoi!" Silver laughed. "You are *red*, Evaris!"

I closed my eyes, feeling lightheaded.

"Oh, come on, don't be dramatic now." He placed a hand on my arm.

"I'm feeling it too," Boa said. "It's pretty bad today."

"Don't say that," I choked out, my eyes still closed. If *Boa* felt sick, I was gearing up to die.

"Yeah, don't freak her out," Silver scolded.

I forced my eyes open, and my vision whirled as I looked around. Despite the dizziness, I fumbled for my glass and downed another gulp. It didn't matter how bad this dose was. I needed to keep up.

As I set the glass down, my arms shook, and I accidentally splashed some leftover juice on my arm. It burned a little. I scratched the point of contact.

My head started spinning, even after I closed my eyes again. It was as if I'd just sat down after running in circles for hours. My head ached from an indescribable pressure, and I gripped the edge of the table, just as I had done during the first dose we took in month one. Every noise in the room seemed to blur together into one deep, howling wind.

The poison would snatch me this time, wouldn't it? I'd pass out and fall from my chair. The next time I'd open my eyes, I'd be in Vakoi City Hospital with my parents at my bedside, eager to say, *I told you so*.

"Antiserum." My voice entered the blur of noise, but I couldn't hear it. I had to trust that I'd spoken at all. "I need it."

"You know—shouldn't—it," Silver said. Some of his words I couldn't make out, but the message was clear from his tone of voice: *Don't take the antiserum.*

"You—fine." It was Boa speaking this time. "If—bad."

When I opened my eyes again, everything was black.

Perhaps my panicked expression freaked them out, because soon enough, someone forced a vial of lukewarm antiserum into my shaky grip. If Boa and Silver had handed it to me, then they no longer trusted that I'd pull through. I wasn't concerned about falling behind anymore either. I'd catch up somehow—maybe I could ask Blimmery for extra doses. Between falling behind and passing out, the lesser evil was crystal clear.

I popped off the cork stopper and braced myself for the taste of vinegar.

A trainee started running in my direction as I brought the vial to my lips. It wasn't Boa or Silver; I could feel them beside me, their shoulders brushing mine. Was it Krevall, hoping to knock the antiserum out of my hands just in time to sabotage me?

I shoved the vial to my lips. The fluid met my tongue just as a force knocked me off my feet, throwing the antiserum out of my hands.

Boa and Silver gasped.

The next thing I knew, I lay sprawled on the marble floor, my vision fading in and out. Hovering right above me was Avarium, panting, staring with a look of concern I'd never seen her wear before. The vial she'd knocked out of my hands had shattered beside me, its yellow fluid oozing into a puddle. My nose wrinkled at the scent of mustard and vinegar.

Avarium knelt and struggled to lift me. Boa skeptically stepped forward to assist her.

Once I was standing, supported by their arms, I looked over at Krevall, who sat at his usual table with a vial of antiserum. This dose had given him shaky arms and quivering eyes, but instead of making himself vomit as he'd planned, he squinted at Avarium.

He had seen her protect me from what should have been safe.

My eyes watered as Krevall tilted his vial, pouring the yellow fluid into his salad bowl. He had put the pieces together: Avarium had poisoned the antiserum, thinking he'd be the only one to take it.

My roommate gripped my arm tighter. Her gray eyes were cold as she stared back at him, but I could feel the tremor in her hand.

Avarium, I thought to myself, *what have you done?*

CHAPTER 11

PIN

Day 78 | 10 trainees remaining

♫ NOBODY'S SAVIOUR · ROWENA WISE ♫

Cal is short for Calamity. Seriously. She told me this while I packed to move out of Room 4. As of yesterday, ten of us remained, leaving one trainee per quarter—no need for roommates anymore.

I hauled a stack of uniform sets out of my dresser. My vision was blurry from today's dose, and being on my feet exhausted me, but I was recovering surprisingly well considering I hadn't taken the antiserum. It was good to know I hadn't truly needed it.

"My parents aren't good with big words," Avarium explained as I tossed another stack of uniforms onto my bed. "They just thought Calamity sounded nice."

It was the first time she had volunteered personal information. I wondered if she felt guilty for nearly poisoning me. *Hopefully.* I had no reason to thank her for saving me from her own trap. She shouldn't have messed with the antiserum in the first place.

If only I had waited longer to drink my juice. Then Krevall would have taken the antiserum before I'd tried to take mine. He'd be hospitalized, and we'd be safe.

"I guess Calamity is a nice name," Avarium added, "if you don't think about what it means."

I paused my packing to glare at her. She was trying to pull a trick, wasn't she? Trying to endear herself to me so I wouldn't be so pissed. Well, it wasn't working.

"For as long as I can remember, I've insisted on *Cal*. Only my family knows what it stands for. And now, you." She ignored my expression, smiling a little. "It still feels like a secret."

"Your name?" I asked dryly.

Avarium's suggestion of a smile faded. "The fact that I bring disaster wherever I go."

I scoffed. "Sounds like a superstition."

"More like a curse." She diverted her gaze to the glass balcony door, her eyes tracing the trees that encompassed the Academy field like a cage. Once again, I wondered if she was referring to Chima. I wondered what it might feel like to fear someone enough to kill them.

I recalled what Silver had told me on our first day, about how she'd struck a log against Chima's head over and over. Perhaps she had a tendency to take things too far, as she'd done today.

I shook off what little empathy I felt and grabbed the last of my uniform sets.

"You could have hurt me." I didn't spare a glance. "You could have hurt *any* of us. Even Boa took the dose hard today. If he needed the antiserum instead, you wouldn't have interfered. You would have let an innocent person get filtered. You're no better than Krevall."

"Boa's weak," Avarium said.

"Excuse me?" I pivoted to face her. "He's not weak."

"Okay." She sat cross-legged on her bed and leaned back against her pillows. In her hands was that mysterious silver stopwatch. She clearly didn't care about making amends anymore.

"You could've at least warned me before lunch. Then you wouldn't have rushed over." I snatched a few books from my desk and tossed them onto my bed. "Now Krevall knows you tried to poison him."

She flipped the stopwatch over in her hand. "You can't tell me what I should and shouldn't do."

My face burned, and despite my better judgment, I shouted back. "What is your *problem*, Avarium?"

I struggled to keep my breathing under control, and she did too—but for a different reason. I didn't notice her eyes were watering until she sniffled and lowered her head.

Before I knew it, she was crying.

Avarium, crying. I couldn't believe it.

Perhaps I couldn't trust her, and those crocodile tears were an act to fool me. Despite knowing this, I couldn't help but soften my voice.

"He doesn't know that I'm aware of his sabotage. That can help us," I said. "But we need to work as a team from now on."

As I crossed to her side of the room, Avarium wiped her tears and looked up at me. The bluish rings under her eyes caught my attention for the first time. Perhaps I hadn't noticed them before because I'd never fully seen her as a real girl like me.

"I was locked up for four months," she said, her voice hardly more than a whisper.

I sat on the end of her bed and listened.

"When I was younger, Professor Embre visited my school. She saw me running and gave me this." Avarium rubbed her thumb over her stopwatch. "So when I saw her in the Detainment Facility, passing my cell, I thought that maybe—if she remembered—I could convince her to help give me a second chance."

I gulped.

"I told her I'd work hard," she continued, "that I'd be the best trainee she's ever seen. I already had the scores and athletic records to prove it. So she vouched for me. Saved my life."

Goosebumps covered my arms. They'd planned to execute her.

Avarium curled her fingers, strangling the ticking stopwatch. "If I don't make the final five," she said, voice tight, "I don't get to go home, Evaris."

My eyes widened as the horror struck me all at once. The guardians wouldn't show mercy on her twice.

"Don't worry, Cal." I reached out, taking her hands in mine. "You're getting out of here alive."

It was the first time I didn't call her *Avarium*.

After moving into my new room that evening, I left for the library to play chess—I needed to keep up appearances.

No one was there, though. I surveyed the other floors until I found Boa, Silver, and Nash in the training room, practicing with primary tools. Gup was there too, on the opposite side of the room, keeping his distance.

Commander Roz had introduced us to dual swords, bows, and throwing blades a couple of weeks ago. Every guardian had a primary tool—and even as trainees, we'd have to commit to one of them soon. Silver had already made his choice: dual swords. He practiced with them now, looping through a sequence Commander Roz had taught him. The strikes and blocks were faster than he could manage, which made him look sloppy. No one bothered to tell him.

"Evaris!" Boa called, waving me over. He pointed to a target, which three throwing stars had pierced. Then he pointed to another, which had three arrows jammed into it. All six were an equal distance from the red bullseyes.

"Which tool do you think I'm better at?"

I shrugged. "Looks like you've been practicing both equally."

"Well, of course. I need to figure out which one comes more naturally."

"Nothing comes naturally. It's all practice. Just pick one and get on with it already."

Boa turned his back to me, studying the two targets, unwilling to consider my advice.

Silver wrapped up a sequence and shared a smile with me. Boa could be so dramatic sometimes.

Beside Silver, Nash released his bowstring, shooting an arrow across the room. It struck the bullseye.

I leaned toward Boa and whispered, "Where's Krevall?"

He gave me a disgusted look. "Why?"

I narrowed my eyes.

"You're always looking at him," he added.

"It's not like that."

"That thing with Avarium was weird too." He picked up the bow he'd been using earlier and aimed at a target. "Why did she ruin your antiserum? Was she trying to sabotage you?"

"Who knows what she was thinking?" I said, acting oblivious.

"His salad turned brown." Nash landed another perfect shot and made eye contact with me.

I froze. "Huh?"

Even Gup, from across the room, stopped throwing darts and looked our way.

"Krevall poured the antiserum onto his salad, and I saw the leaves crinkle up," Nash explained. "In a few seconds, they turned brown. Mustard seed and vinegar don't do that. I told Doctor Blimmery, and he brought in a fresh set of antiserum vials. Said it looked like belladonna."

Silver's jaw dropped into an open-mouth grin. "Avarium put belladonna in the antiserum?"

"She wouldn't do that!" I exclaimed.

"How would *you* know?" Boa crossed his arms. "Unless you're hiding something. Like the fact that you're friends."

"We're *not* friends."

Gup started throwing darts harder than earlier, stealing my attention just briefly.

"She wanted to protect you," Silver said.

"Don't be ridiculous," I snapped. "I have no clue what happened at lunch, okay?"

Boa and Silver seemed skeptical. They said nothing more before resuming their practice—but Nash continued to stare at me. I could taste the tension in the air.

I fled the training room with a quick *goodnight*.

The next day, during recreation time, I waited for the boys to arrive for their afternoon run.

Krevall was first to show. He joined me in the courtyard by the statue of Emperor Vakoi and gazed up at it. Doctor Blimmery had told us that this statue represented every emperor in the Vakoi family lineage, which was easily believable—it looked nothing like the real Emperor Vakoi, whom I had seen a handful of times at Palace events that the Starfalls had been graciously invited to. How silly it was that this one statue represented all these different men. Were they the same in mind?

"Incredible. Wish I had my glasses right now," Krevall said. A moment later, he dropped his chin to make eye contact with me. "Have you met the Emperor, being from Vakoi City and all?"

I pointed to the statue that didn't represent the current Emperor's stockier frame. "*This* Emperor?"

He nodded, and I shrugged. I could tell he wanted to ask questions, but thankfully, Silver and Nash showed up, their eyebrows rising at the sight of me.

"What are you doing here?" Silver asked. He seemed a little agitated.

"What do you think?" I replied. "I'm finally taking you up on your offer to run."

"You're not sick?" Nash asked Krevall and me. "Neither of you took the antiserum yesterday."

"We'll take it slow," I assured him.

"That's right," Krevall said. "Might fall behind you two." Our eyes locked; he understood that I was here to talk.

We split into pairs. I ran beside Krevall, wishing I were anywhere but *with* Krevall, doing anything but running.

"Look," I said, nearly breathless. "I know what you've done."

He stomped onward, panting. "What do you mean?"

"The essay, the uniforms, the flowers, the horse, the boots, the rabbit—"

"What—"

"Don't play stupid."

I stared onward, but I could feel his gaze burning through me.

"You helped her," he said, his voice hardly audible in the wind.

"I told her not to do it."

"She could have killed me."

I shuffled to a stop, and he did too, his face reddening. I wanted to call him a hypocrite, but I couldn't deny that Cal had crossed a line he hadn't. At worst, he had killed a horse that was scheduled to die the next day anyway. Everything else he'd done was purely psychological.

I needed to trust that he had *some* morals, considering what I was about to do.

"I'm sorry," I said, despite the words doing everything they could to stay inside my mouth. "I should've made sure that she wouldn't go behind my back."

Krevall narrowed his eyes, knowing there had to be more.

There was.

"But you can't sabotage her," I said. "Go after anyone else—hell, go after me—but not her."

He tilted his head. "Why?"

"Krevall," I said, "if Cal doesn't make the final five, the Force will reinstate her execution."

He broke a smile.

"I'm serious," I said.

"The guardians wouldn't do that. She's lying to you, has you wrapped around her finger."

"Think about it. Why would the Force send her straight from the Detainment Facility to the Academy? This is the only use they have for her. They pardoned her, but they didn't set her free."

"That's a stretch."

I stepped closer. "I know how badly you want this job, and I'm not saying you need to protect her. I'm saying that if you keep playing dirty, don't pull any tricks on *her*. Play a fair game with *her*."

He stared down at me blankly.

"In exchange, I'll keep her off your back, and I won't tell anyone what you've done."

Still, no expression. I turned to leave, dissatisfaction clawing at my chest. Perhaps my words had gone in one ear and out the other.

"Starfall!" Krevall called before I'd gone too far.

I looked back to see him frowning at me.

"I play dirty, but not *that* dirty. I won't go after Avarium."

My eyes widened.

"And as for that little incident in the dining hall, consider you both forgiven. But learn to keep your dog on a leash."

Despite my efforts to suppress it, a smile found its way to my face.

Krevall smiled back. "Nice move, by the way. Didn't see that coming."

I sensed he respected me for catching him. And that respect made me trust him more, even if just a little. My parents had always told me that playing ignorant could only work in my favor, and yet here I had chosen honesty, and honesty had prevailed.

The trainee had only taken a few sips of juice before falling out of his chair.

Cal screamed as he toppled onto the marble floor. She rushed over and dropped to feel for a pulse.

The other eight of us gathered next.

"He's not moving," Silver noted.

Boa crouched and shook the boy's shoulder. "Hey, wake up!"

Silver ran off to fetch Doctor Blimmery, while the rest of the boys rushed for the antiserum. They thought the dose was too high and would take them out next.

Cal and I lingered by the body. We made eye contact, then looked across the dining hall at Krevall.

He stared back as he brought a vial of yellow fluid to his lips, making himself vomit even though he knew he didn't have to.

Beside him, Nash's face twisted in guilt. He turned away, breaking under our glares, and clenched his eyes shut. In a single motion, he chugged a vial and vomited too.

Silver returned with Doctor Blimmery quickly—and just as quickly, the guardian announced Daxel Guppy dead.

CHAPTER 12

ENDGAME

Day 80 | 9 trainees remaining

♫ FALLEN LEAVES - HUNTER AS A HORSE ♫

Cal Avarium handed me a shovel. The guardians only gave us five. Avarium, Silver, and I—along with two more boys—handled the digging. Krevall, Nash, Boa, and one other trainee stood back and watched. It was better that way. Krevall didn't deserve to be anywhere near Gup's grave.

We worked in the woods just outside the Academy field, as the guardians had instructed. Their looming silhouettes watched us from the courtyard. I wanted to ask why they weren't sending his body home. What would they tell Gup's family?

But they were too far and too furious to receive questions. I could only channel my confusion into my shovel as we dug, and dug, and dug. It was the repetition that tore me down. Before I knew it, the wooden handle had splintered my palms, and the prickling pain pushed me over the edge. I hurled another pile of dirt aside, letting out a surge of bubbling sobs.

For a long moment, the echo of my grief was all that filled the woods.

Avarium stopped digging to set a hand on my shoulder. I wished I could wrap my arms around her and relish in the subtle gesture. Why were these boys all stone-faced, staring at me like I was having a meltdown for no reason? Krevall had killed one of our own. Why weren't the guardians doing anything? Why weren't *we* doing anything?

I sensed movement in my peripheral vision and shook Avarium's hand off my shoulder. In the distance, Professor Embre had left Commander Roz and Doctor Blimmery. She made her way toward us from across the field. Silver and the two other boys stopped digging.

"Wipe your tears, Evaris. You're pissing Professor Embre off." Silver's voice was firm, but I knew he meant well.

"Sorry," I choked out, drying my face with my sleeves.

"Can you keep going?" he said, softer this time.

I nodded despite every part of me wanting to say no.

Silver gave me a reassuring pat before getting back to work. I readjusted my grip on the shovel and winced. Another boy rushed forward and took it from me.

"It's okay," Nash whispered. "I'll handle it."

He stepped into my place by the soon-to-be grave, forcing me into the line of bystanders.

Krevall bit his lip and blinked a few times, as if holding back tears. I didn't buy it one bit. He had murdered a boy, but his crime was even worse than Avarium's. He had no one to protect but himself.

I planted myself next to him to look like I wasn't afraid—but in truth, I wanted to run. More than I hated him, I loved the thought of being safe. Maybe my parents weren't so bad after all. Maybe I could tolerate life as an ordinary Starfall. Maybe I could even learn to enjoy stitching up suits or boiling worms into silk.

The next time I looked over my shoulder at the field, Professor Embre had rejoined Doctor Blimmery and Commander Roz in the courtyard. She was no longer coming to reprimand me, but I was certain I'd disappointed her. She had vouched for a foolish, sloppy mistake in the end.

When I looked ahead, the grave was dug.

Nash and a few others fetched Gup's body from the dining hall. Some trainees who had been stone-faced earlier wiped their eyes at the sight of him.

Tears stung mine, but I didn't dare break again.

Gup's uniform was still patchy from the sewing job I'd done.

My heart raced as they lowered him into the hole and covered him in dirt, bit by bit. I watched his face disappear under rocks, twigs, beetles, dead leaves...

Eventually, we faced a heaping pile, his body displacing dirt. Would future trainees at the Academy notice, or would they walk over this patch without question?

I waited for someone to lead a makeshift funeral effort. Perhaps we could each volunteer a moment we'd shared with Gup.

But no one did. We just stood there.

The funeral still happened, though. I could feel it in the air. We were all silently remembering our time with him and saying our goodbyes. None of us had befriended Gup, but none of us hated him either. We simply hadn't welcomed him, and now we paid the price.

A crow cawed in the silence.

One by one, the boys left the gravesite. When it was Silver's time, he hugged me and said sorry. I didn't blame him for his harsh words earlier— it beat Professor Embre's wrath. So I said *thank you* to his *I'm sorry*, and that was that.

Then it was just Avarium and me, staring at the mound. I imagined Gup's body down there, still fresh, almost alive. Just hours ago he had breathed among us, and now he didn't exist.

Some boys cried that night. I could hear them through the walls. Footsteps too, as the sleepless ones left their rooms. I saw a trainee at the grave from my new room's balcony when I stepped out for some fresh air. I couldn't make out who it was. Eventually, he turned back, and I went to bed.

I thought of the Underground and how many people they'd harmed in their raids. If anyone was worth killing, it was members of the terrorist group, yet here we were, killing fellow trainees.

Then I thought of Krevall. I had taken a leap of faith to trust him, and he was true to his word. As promised, he didn't go after Cal.

He went after Gup instead.

It occurred to me that maybe, just *maybe*, Gup had died because of me. Perhaps if I hadn't gone to Krevall yesterday, he wouldn't have done this.

Why hadn't I trusted Boa or Silver instead? Even knowing what he'd done, I had sought *Krevall* out and played *his* game.

If a younger version of myself were to watch me now, she would never agree with whom I chose to trust. In trying to win the program, the program had changed me—and not in a good way.

I wrestled out of my blankets and grabbed a notepad from my desk. A system, I decided, could help me determine if Gup's death was my fault or not. So I sat there, cross-legged, brainstorming a tally of sorts.

Every *X* would represent a good deed. Every *O* would represent a bad one.

I would rate each act in isolation, without nuance.

Did I kill Gup?

No.

Did I willingly make a deal with someone bad?

Yes.

I jotted down an *O*. Maybe if I kept count from now on, I wouldn't lose myself completely.

Avarium woke me up with a series of panicked knocks—a kind gesture. Perhaps she worried I would oversleep. The guardians had made it clear, the evening prior, that we were to meet in the courtyard at the crack of dawn.

I hadn't changed into my pajamas last night. I got out of bed still wearing the dirt-stained pants from Gup's burial.

It was still dark when Avarium and I got to the courtyard. *Crack of dawn* wasn't exactly an accurate time. The guardians weren't here yet, but the seven boys were. They weren't even talking. They didn't know who they could or couldn't trust.

Boa fidgeted with a pencil. Silver blinked repeatedly to keep himself awake. Nash seemed to be focused on his breathing.

Among them, Krevall blended right in. His red eyes made my blood boil. I threw away my restraint and held his gaze, right in front of everyone. "You poisoned him."

His lips curved downward. "You really think I'd do something like that?"

I closed the gap between us. He didn't step back.

"Confess," I said, glaring up at him.

"It wasn't me."

I punched him straight in the nose.

Boa gasped as Krevall stumbled back into the statue of Emperor Vakoi. I shot after him, intending to pin him to the structure and land another hit. It didn't matter if I needed to add an extra *O* to the tally in my notepad. I could balance it out with a good deed later.

Silver held me back before I could reach him. "Quit it!"

I struggled against his grip. "Let me go! He murdered him!"

Krevall gathered himself and wiped the blood from his nose. It was such a small droplet. I gritted my teeth, eager to spill more.

As if on cue, another fist met his face, though not my own. Silver loosened his hold, and I stopped fighting back.

Cal had struck Krevall in the face, earning splatters of blood on the white sleeves of her button-up.

He hunched over, gripping his nose tenderly. Nothing but confusion and pain marked his face. *Liar.*

The Academy's front door swung open.

Krevall straightened up. Cal stepped away from him and wiped her hand on her uniform vest.

Professor Embre stormed over. "What the hell is going on here?"

We looked away.

"There was no belladonna in your lunch juice," Doctor Blimmery said, joining her side. "Yet Daxel's glass contained a lethal dose of calabar."

Commander Roz was the last to arrive. "We expect a confession."

Professor Embre led the interrogation first. The nine of us stood in a line as she walked back and forth, asking questions, refuting answers, prying for a confession. One boy interrupted, asking if he could go home. She slapped him in the face for that.

"Which one of you killed him?"

Commander Roz went next, walking up the line and staring us down. When he got to me, I glued my lips shut, forcing myself not to yell that Krevall had done this. They would only take a confession as truth, but did they really believe such intimidation tactics would get them one? If it hadn't worked after the horse-killing, it wouldn't work now.

Hours passed. I shuffled my toes in my boots, sore from standing. My stomach growled. My tongue dried out.

The guardians had stepped aside a few minutes ago. They muttered amongst each other, red-faced and tense, discussing our punishment. It felt like an eternity before they approached us again.

"The nine of you are disastrous." Commander Roz crossed his arms and shook his head. "There is no reason for infighting when the Underground exists."

"A wasted batch," Professor Embre spat. "Pathetic."

"Clearly, the culprit has no intention of leaving." Doctor Blimmery raised his chin. "So, for the rest of you, we offer a choice. If you refuse to remain here with a killer, step forward."

The boy Professor Embre had slapped volunteered first. Another boy followed his lead.

My pulse quickened. I looked over at Krevall, urging him to go home. He could spare us from his wretched presence and get away with everything.

My fear was that he'd stay and *still* get away with everything.

Another boy stepped forward. Six of us remained.

My eyes widened. This was my last chance to filter myself. I could escape this disastrous program and find a new path—whatever that might be.

But if I did, Krevall would make the final five by default.

I wanted to believe the guardians wouldn't accept a killer among the winners, yet they had pardoned Avarium for killing Chima, so what did I know? Maybe this is why Doctor Blimmery had warned me about bad people in the Force. I had no clue how many were already in it, but they couldn't possibly be as dangerous as Krevall. Knowing his pettiness, if I left now, was there even a slim chance he would murder Avarium tomorrow?

And if he did, would her family hear the real news?

Did Gup's family hear the real news?

"Anyone else?" Professor Embre asked.

If I stayed, Krevall would remain a threat to me. But on the bright side, I could buy us more time to get rid of him.

My safety, or *everyone's* safety?

One option was clearly an *X*, while the other was an *O*.

I stood my ground.

"Very well." Professor Embre gestured for the three boys who filtered themselves to follow her to the stable. Commander Roz and Doctor Blimmery stayed back to announce the most unexpected punishment imaginable.

"You will be left at the Academy, just you six, for one week," Commander Roz said. "And when we return, you will be a team."

It was quiet as we processed their decision. I didn't understand the logic.

"What about food?" Nash asked.

"The cooks will come, and they will go, as they always do," said Doctor Blimmery.

I froze. Why would they leave us unattended when the culprit likely remained?

It was the Cal Avarium question all over again. Why allow a murderer into the program?

Finally, despite the rumors, and what Avarium had told me herself, I found the answer—Cal Avarium was here because the guardians tolerated murder. Because the guardians often *did* murder, and perhaps that was something they were looking for too.

They were not furious that one of us had killed. They were furious that one of us had killed without permission. That was the real problem.

The guardians want us to be a team.

They don't care if we murder.

They're leaving us unsupervised for a reason.

This wasn't a week to rekindle our warm, fuzzy feelings for each other, was it? This was a week to identify the team of five within the unsteady six.

This was our final filtration:
Permission to kill.

CHAPTER 13

CHECK

Day 81 | 6 trainees remaining

♫ LOOK ALIVE - HANA VU ♫

Cal Avarium was nowhere to be found. While the rest of us watched our instructors escort the filtered boys off the grounds, my ex-roommate had slipped into Belladonna Guardian Academy. We didn't even realize she was gone until we turned to head inside.

Krevall and Nash quickened their pace, scaling the front steps first. The sight of Krevall's back made my fingers roll into fists. I had never struck someone out of rage before. My knuckles were still sore, but I would have gladly broken my hand to watch him suffer even more.

Boa grabbed my arm as Krevall and Nash walked through the main door. I didn't resist him. Despite my eagerness for blood, I wouldn't be reckless. There were no guardians to save us now.

Perhaps there had never been.

A moment later, Boa let go. We stood in the courtyard with Silver for a minute, staring up at the Academy. We hadn't even gone back inside, yet it already felt emptier than ever. The wind howled around us.

I kept my eyes peeled and my ears open as we entered the building, trying to sense where Krevall and Nash were located. Luckily, when we reached the lobby on the second floor, I heard them mumbling in the old room they used to share, their words unidentifiable.

Silver and I found ourselves in Boa's quarter. We spent what felt like an hour without saying a word. I pulled my notepad out of my pocket and stared at the *O* from last night, which represented my choice to trust Krevall. I used one of Boa's pencils to scribble an *O* for punching him, because while it felt right, nuance aside, it was objectively bad to hurt someone. Then I added an *X* for choosing to stay. Two bad deeds, one good one. It was relieving to know where I stood.

I stole a guardian memoir from Boa's desk and sat cross-legged on his bed with the pages in my lap. I kept rereading paragraphs because I couldn't comprehend them. My mind always drifted back to Gup.

I saw a trainee, dead on the floor.

Poisonous juice spilling out of a toppled glass.

Krevall, observing the scene with his hollow eyes.

I didn't deserve to say that I missed Gup. I hardly spoke to him. But I missed the line Krevall crossed when he poisoned him. Now even the worst-case scenarios felt possible. Who would he kill next?

My grip on the book tightened, my breaths quickening. I couldn't focus on the words. Cal was alone right now, the most vulnerable among us. Was she in her room, behind a locked door, or was she out in the open, waiting to be sacrificed?

"Hey." Boa, sitting next to me, set a hand on my shoulder.

I shook his arm off and darted for the door, leaving the book behind. I needed to check on her.

Silver slipped in front of me, blocking my way to the exit.

"We should stay close." His voice was deeper than usual. "Avarium is—"

I scoffed before he could finish, my face burning. "You think *she* killed him? It was Krevall, okay?"

"Was *not*," Silver said, shaking his head.

"Was too!" I exclaimed. "And he's the one who dug up that rabbit, killed my horse, and—"

"Do you have proof?" Boa asked from across the room.

"Seriously? You're pushing for a confession too?" I looked back and forth between them. "It's simple. Who do you trust more? Me, or Krevall?"

Silver sighed.

"Honestly, Evaris," Boa said, "trust goes both ways, and you haven't said a word to us until now."

My objection clotted in my throat. He was right. Why should they trust me when I had hidden the truth for so long? I'd been too proud—too afraid of the idea that they might not believe me.

"Every time we asked why you were acting weird, you always brushed it off." Silver narrowed his eyes. "How are we supposed to know that you're not blaming your own crime on Krevall?"

My jaw dropped. It was one thing to call out my behavior, but to accuse *me* of killing Gup?

"Move," I muttered, my voice hardly more than a whisper.

His eyes widened. "Look, I didn't mean that, okay?"

I pushed my way past him and rushed through the door. Finding Cal wasn't even on my mind anymore. I just needed to get away.

"Evaris!" he called.

My legs moved on their own, carrying me down to the first floor and through the courtyard. I didn't stop running until I'd crossed the field to Gup's grave.

I dropped to my knees by the mound of fresh dirt, panting, wishing Krevall hadn't messed with that boot. I would've been eliminated during the sparring filtration. I'd be safe at home right now.

But I can't go home.

I placed a hand on the mound of dirt. It was cold in the shade.

"They don't believe me, Gup," I whispered.

I had found myself here, perhaps because a part of me knew this grave was the only thing keeping me tethered. I couldn't allow Gup's killer to get away with this. Even though I so badly wanted someone else to be the hero, I needed to stay and win—so Krevall would lose. And if I didn't have help from Boa and Silver, then I would do it alone. Whatever it'd take.

I flinched when a hand gripped my shoulder. For some reason, I expected

Cal, but I looked up at Silver.

"Tell us everything, start to finish," he said, "and I'll believe you."

Tears welled in my eyes when he knelt and pulled me into a hug.

I melted into his arms, wishing I wasn't pathetic enough to need them.

Lunch was served at the usual time. Boa, Silver, and I arrived at the dining hall early to ensure that Krevall couldn't tamper with our trays. I had explained *everything*, and they had not taken the information lightly.

Luckily, Krevall and Nash didn't show up for lunch. Neither did Cal. I wondered if she was hungry, so I grabbed an extra tray, hoping I'd find her in Room 4.

Boa and Silver seemed hesitant to knock on her door. I couldn't do it, with both hands occupied.

"Are you sure about her?" Silver asked me.

Boa paced the lobby. "How do you know she's not working with him?" He put his hands in his pockets, then took them out again. "What if they're secretly in cahoots?"

"Please..." I was truly pleading. "Give her a chance. I trust her."

It was the first time I'd blatantly stood up for Cal in front of them. And it amazed me how quickly it seemed to calm them down.

Silver took a deep breath and finally knocked on her door.

"It's Evaris," I said, so she wouldn't panic.

Cal cracked the door open and peered through, her eyes widening, gray pupils floating in a sea of white. She looked at Boa, then Silver, then me.

"Hey." I offered a tray. "Can we come in?"

She took the meal and stepped aside, studying Boa and Silver as they slipped into her room. I sat on my old bed, but they stood around, hesitant to make themselves comfortable.

Silver flinched when Cal locked the door behind him.

"Eat on the floor," she said.

Boa and Silver frowned at each other.

I couldn't help but chuckle. "She just doesn't want crumbs on the beds."

In truth, I had no clue what her actual reasoning was. I just didn't want them to be more skeptical than they already were. Trusting me didn't equate to trusting her.

The four of us gathered on the floor in a circle, trays spread out in front of us. Boa waited until Silver started eating forkfuls of salad before he took his first bite. Perhaps he was paranoid that Krevall had somehow poisoned our food before it reached the serving table.

I shook the idea away and took a bite myself. "Cal," I said, feeling responsible for leading the conversation, "I told them everything."

Not one emotion crossed her face. I couldn't place whether she was silently furious or didn't care at all.

"We still don't know if Nash is involved," Boa added.

"But we should keep our distance from both of them, just in case," Silver said, "and try to hold out until the guardians return. Then we can explain what Krevall did."

"They won't believe us," Cal and I said in unison. We met eyes. Had she tried to speak with the guardians too?

"It's the word of four trainees against two at most," Silver countered. "They'll at least investigate."

"No. We need to kill him." Cal took a bite.

Boa and Silver stared in horror. We understood our instructors would likely tolerate a kill this week, but that did not mean someone *had* to die.

"*Kill* him?" Boa whispered. "Are you crazy?"

Cal whispered back, "He killed Gup."

I wanted Krevall gone more than anything, but perhaps next week there'd be a filtration, and he would lose fair and square. We had no reason to stoop to his level.

Boa and Silver squinted at Cal. Clearly, they weren't ready to say yes.

But none of us said no.

I found it exceptionally difficult to be alone during Dead Week—as our group of four had soon dubbed it.

We were used to the Academy feeling much too large for us, so having fewer trainees around wasn't what made it *dead*. It was the lack of a schedule. We went from spending most of our days taking notes, studying, working with plants, drinking poison, recovering from poison, sparring with tools, practicing horseback formations, and the like... only to suddenly do nothing but fear for our lives.

Krevall only appeared with Nash to grab food every other meal or so. Even then, he never spoke to us, never even *looked* at us. I was certain, by how thin our walls were, that he heard our group chatting in Room 4 and knew we were on the same team now. But instead of acting afraid of being outnumbered, he minded his own business.

He was planning something. Certainly.

On our second day, Cal and I had gathered tools from the training room. Every bow, sword, and throwing blade had its place, so we easily noticed a bow was missing, along with three quivers of arrows and a pair of dual swords. Those were Krevall's and Nash's favorites.

We took everything else and loaded it into Room 4. This required several trips up and down that left my arms sore. It was strange that Krevall hadn't fully cleared out the training room, since he'd gotten to it first. It almost felt like he'd left some tools behind to mock us.

Boa and Silver spent that same day fetching water from the fountain downstairs in canisters and oil jars they'd washed in the kitchen. We wanted to do everything possible to reduce the time spent outside Cal's quarter. We even put extra clothes from our rooms in her dressers, since we were spending all our time there anyway.

When we didn't have any tasks, our thoughts wandered into sick places. We double-checked the locks on the door and moved a desk in front of it when all four of us were inside. The balcony was a constant source of paranoia—an arrow from the field could easily shatter its glass door, and there were vines on that side of the building, so a trainee could theoretically climb up to this room.

Boa tried to predict Krevall's plan, just like he'd tried to predict filtrations. He dragged me to the Medical lab—a calculated risk, he'd explained—to see if Krevall had taken anything.

All of Doctor Blimmery's calabar beans were gone.

Once again, Krevall's plan involved poison. We took the vials of belladonna serum so we could combat the toxins if they ever entered our system, considering how the two plants canceled each other out.

Boa and I also brought books from the library that day, plus a chessboard, to help keep our minds busy. When we got bored of books and games, sometimes we'd lie on the floor to chat about our old lives, and how we might kill Krevall, and whether we *should* kill Krevall, and back to our old lives again.

Apparently, Silver had grown up on the southern coast. His father was a fisherman who sold his catch at the local market. It sounded impressive, how Silver would help him on the boats and the docks.

"I don't even like the taste of fish that much." He chuckled. "But the ocean is something else. I used to go out with the other kids, and we'd dive into the water, try to catch fish by hand."

"Swimming in the *ocean?*" Boa shuddered. "People die out there. All it takes is one big wave to—"

"Worrying is a distraction," Cal butted in. She was stretching again, as if this were any other day in the program. I stopped playing a boring game of chess against myself and frowned at her. Once we handled Krevall, maybe I could give her some social tips. Unlike me, Boa and Silver hadn't spent the last few months warming up to her brashness.

"How about you, Boa?" I leaned back on the floor and propped myself up with my arms. "What kind of farm did you grow up on?"

"How'd you know it was a farm?"

"You know horses," Cal answered for me.

A smile appeared, but he suppressed it. Perhaps receiving a compliment from her confused him.

"Livestock," Boa answered.

"So just... a bunch of animals?" I asked.

"Animals for food. I've killed plenty of chickens."

It was Silver's turn to shudder. "Fish aren't fleshy and squelchy like mammals are."

Boa laughed to himself. "You know, there's this coming-of-age tradition in my family to have a pet chicken for a few months. You name it. Take it with you everywhere you go. And then one night, they bring you out to the yard, hand you a knife, and tell you it's time for supper."

"That's funny," Cal said, though she didn't even smile.

I asked Boa and Silver more questions about their upbringings. How big were their towns? Did they have any siblings? What were their schools like, their old teachers and classmates? It surprised me when they stopped discussing themselves and turned their focus to Cal.

"Did you really kill Chima?" asked Silver.

She nodded.

"Was it really a log?" asked Boa.

She nodded again.

"Do you regret it?" It was I who had asked, and my question caught me by surprise.

"No," Cal said. "He would've killed my brother. Maybe not then, in the woods that day. But someday. People like him don't stop until someone *else* stops *them*."

It went quiet again. But I sensed, in the silence, a cautious understanding.

On our fifth day of Dead Week, Boa insisted we stop eating.

"It's a good precaution," he explained. "We can survive just fine without food until the guardians return. It made sense to eat earlier in the week, but now that we've made it this far, why risk a poisoning?"

We agreed with him, though we *dis*agreed by the following evening. Silver claimed we needed to be sharp and alert, in case Krevall attacked.

"No," Boa said, as though he believed himself to be our group leader.

I couldn't sleep that night. My stomach growled and caved in.

Silver, from his pile of pillows and blankets on the floor, complained about his hunger too. But in no time, the exhaustion took him under, and he started snoring. *Lucky.*

I tossed over in my old bed and could feel my insides churning.

"Psst!"

I pushed myself up into a seated position.

"Are you still hungry?" Cal whispered.

I smiled and stepped over Boa's sleeping body. Cal opened her desk drawer and produced the lock busters that Boa and Silver had used to sneak into the kitchen.

We moved the desk that blocked the door aside and slipped into the lobby. Perhaps it was foolish to leave, but Krevall was likely asleep at this hour. And after six days of nothing happening, I was starting to believe he'd only taken those weapons and calabar beans in self-defense.

We traveled downstairs and into the dining hall. Right past the serving table was the door to the kitchen. Cal handed me the lock busters and watched as I fiddled with its pieces unsuccessfully. *For the glory of Vakoi, I hate these things.*

"You do it." I offered the tool back.

She shook her head. "No."

I frowned, expecting an explanation, but she didn't need to give me one. We were at the Academy, and there were certain skills the graduates would need. Maybe she was right to push me.

I fiddled around for five more minutes, cursing to myself, before the binding lock finally clicked.

The kitchen was small, about the size of the infirmary, with beautiful stoves. Cal approached a latched door in the ground, near one corner, which led to an underground cellar. We used the ladder to climb down into it.

It was dark and cold. Cal lit a handheld lantern that she'd brought with her so we could survey the uncooked meats. We brought our steak slices back up to the kitchen.

Cal did the cooking. Admittedly, I had never cooked *anything*, so I thanked her.

We talked about the future. She had been doing that a lot these past few days. She hadn't really done that before.

"When we get out of here," she said, buttering an iron pan, "I'm going to work toward becoming the youngest unit leader in guardian history."

I grinned. It was nice to hear her dream a little.

"Two years and two months," she continued. "That's the current record.

Not too hard to beat, I think."

"And what's so cool about being a unit leader?"

She thought for a while before giving me an answer. "It just means that you're dedicated, a bit more than everyone else."

I thought of how hard she had worked in the program so far. I wondered if I could ever be as dedicated as she was about *anything*.

"How do you like your steak cooked?" she asked.

"All the way," I replied.

"I like my steak raw."

I nearly gasped, and she cracked a smile.

"Just kidding."

This time, I really *did* gasp. "Cal Avarium is a jokester?"

"I'm all sorts."

"Oh, is that so?"

"So!"

The sound of footsteps just outside the kitchen door made us flinch. We ducked behind the stove, though it was pointless. Clearly, there was steak cooking. Cal grabbed a knife from a lower cabinet; I grabbed a pan.

I closed my eyes at the sound of clinking lock busters. The noise didn't last long; the person outside realized the door was already open.

I gritted my teeth as the hinges creaked. Boa and Silver were deep sleepers. I doubted one of them would go off looking for us alone.

As soon as the intruder stepped inside, Cal leaped to her feet, knife drawn. "Stay back!"

"Whoa! Hey, hey!"

It wasn't Krevall.

I stood, my eyes widening at the sight of Nash, hands raised in surrender. "I'm just here to get some food."

Cal waved her knife at him. "Grab it and go."

Nash looked at me, then back at Cal. He crept to a shelving unit and grabbed a few mangoes.

"Krevall's been planning something." He slid the fruit into his book bag. "Tomorrow night, I'll be in the field with my bow. Get him onto the balcony, and I'll handle the rest."

I frowned. Was I interpreting this right? Was Nash offering to help?

He stopped packing and lowered his voice. "It wasn't supposed to kill him."

Cal eased her grip on the knife. I thought of Nash's guilty expression after Gup's death. He had known Krevall's plan and let it happen. No wonder he took the shovel for me. He was trying to make up for it. Still was.

"Why not murder Krevall yourself?" Cal asked.

"I just..." With a shake of his head, Nash gathered a few more mangoes from the shelves. "I don't want to be close when it happens."

"You're a coward," she said.

"Maybe." He finished packing and rushed to the door.

"Hey," I called.

Nash looked back, gripping his bag with one hand to keep the fruit from overflowing.

"Thanks," I said. Partially for turning against Krevall, and partially for taking the shovel.

He nodded once, his expression hardening. "Balcony. Don't forget."

CHAPTER 14

CHECKMATE

Day 87 | 6 trainees remaining

♫ IF I WAS DEAD - BROOKE BENTHAM ♫

Cal Avarium didn't believe him. "If Nash wanted to help," she said, "he would've given us a tip earlier."

"I'm hungry," Silver muttered from the floor. He lay on a mess of blankets with an arm draped over his eyes to block the morning light.

"What if it's a trick, and they're actually working together?" Boa paced the room, hands folded under his chin. "Maybe Krevall sent Nash to the kitchen to give us a *fake* tip."

I rolled my eyes. "You're both being paranoid. They couldn't have known that we'd be in the kitchen." I nudged Silver with my boot. "Come on, back up here, Big Tooth."

"Hungry," he repeated. Cal and I should have brought back more than a few handfuls of packaged crackers, but we'd been too concerned about running into Krevall last night.

Boa snatched one of the packages from my old nightstand and tossed it at Silver. The crackers landed next to him on his wrinkled blankets.

"Eat up," Boa said. "We need your help."

Silver turned onto his side and blinked at the food. "But I ate most of them already..."

"I don't need it." Boa looked away, fidgeting with his hands. "Besides, I'm the one who suggested we stop eating."

Silver didn't protest again. He sat up, broke into the package, and stuffed a whole cracker into his mouth. "Well, I agree with Evaris," he said as he chewed. "Let's trust Nash and get Krevall onto the balcony."

I leaned my head back in relief. Out of the four of us, Silver had spent the most time with Nash—he'd gone on runs with him almost every day. If Silver trusted him, I felt more confident about doing the same.

Cal raised her voice, unconvinced. "Krevall and Nash killed Gup. We can't trust either of them."

I sat next to her on the bed. "Nash wasn't involved."

"Either way, we don't need his help." She narrowed her eyes. "It's four against one—two, at most. We can easily kill Krevall on our own."

Silver sighed. "I don't know, Avarium."

Boa started pacing again. "What if the guardians aren't actually okay with it? What if we get punished?"

"That won't happen," Cal said.

"Just three months ago, you were locked up," I muttered.

Boa nodded and pointed at me. "And don't forget that Krevall took calabar beans from the lab. It could be more dangerous to fight him than we think." He stopped and made eye contact with each of us, his voice firmer now. "I say we block up the door and hide out until morning."

Silver swallowed his last bite of crackers. "I'm sure Krevall expects us to block the door. He probably has a plan to get us anyway. Maybe through the balcony or something. We can't expect to hide anymore."

"Exactly," I said. "Trusting Nash is our safest option. Even if he doesn't shoot like he said he would, we can push Krevall down as a last resort."

"Maybe that's exactly what they want." Boa gestured at the glass door. "As soon as one of us steps out to finish the job, Nash shoots *them*. They might not even care who it is."

Cal scoffed. "You're all dancing around what needs to be done."

"We're being cautious," I said, my face running hot. "Krevall trusts Nash, okay? He expects *us* to fight back, but he won't expect his friend to shoot him. We can use that to our advantage."

"You're just scared." A pause. "That's okay. I'll handle it myself."

"Cal," I warned through gritted teeth. "We need to work as a team from now on, remember?"

She stared at me with dead eyes. I sensed zero remorse for how she'd almost poisoned me. She wanted Krevall gone, even if it endangered us. What if he retaliated against her impulsive attack by killing Boa, Silver, or *me*? How could I trust that Cal's rogue actions wouldn't backfire once more?

Nash had given us a way to get one step ahead of Krevall, and Cal refused to take it.

"As soon as he gets here," she said, "I'm killing him."

Time dripped away slowly on our last day of Dead Week. I wished it would pour, yet I also wished it would freeze. What a perfect definition of dread.

Boa kept losing motivation before the endgame—his favorite part of our chess matches. It was becoming harder to distract ourselves from Krevall's imminent plan. Plus, being hungry *and* thirsty didn't help. Our canisters and jars were running low on water, but no pair among us wanted to risk leaving Room 4. We counted and rationed our sips instead.

In the early evening, I rested on my old bed and stared at Cal for a while. She stood by the door, her silver stopwatch in one hand and a dagger in the other. Nothing could change her mind.

Silver lay down next to me. "What are you thinking about?" he whispered.

I rolled onto my side to face him. "Gup," I replied, though that wasn't quite the real answer. I was thinking about what death might feel like. Was it anything like the darkness I'd entered before almost passing out from our belladonna doses? Was it similar to the moment I'd lost consciousness before my concussion, minus the feeling of waking up?

I hoped I wouldn't find out tonight.

As the sun set, we selected our tools.

Cal secured a bandolier of throwing blades—darts and stars—across her chest.

Boa slung a bow over his shoulder, along with a quiver of arrows. Finally, he made his choice.

Silver grabbed a set of dual swords while I settled on a dagger—every guardian's secondary tool. I preferred the bow as a primary, but this early into the program, I knew daggers best.

We stashed our remaining tools in the restroom and dragged my old dresser to block its door. Krevall could easily move it to access our spares, but that would take several seconds, and time could buy us our lives.

Boa tried to block the main door with Cal's desk, but the three of us stopped him. Silver and I needed Krevall to enter so we could get him to the balcony and follow Nash's plan. Avarium wanted Krevall to enter so she could murder him on the spot.

All we did was lock the door. Not to keep him out, but to hear him coming.

I crept to the balcony and peered through the glass. It was too dark outside to spot Nash and his bow. I could only hope he was down there as he'd claimed.

Cal planted herself by the main door, a shiny throwing dart at the ready. I motioned for her to join me against the wall a greater distance away. She shook her head.

Boa nestled into the corner farthest from the door, an arrow already in place. I doubted he would shoot.

Silver stuck beside me with a sword in each hand. I brushed his arm, and he offered me a quick smile. The fear hid behind his glistening eyes.

Together, the four of us faced the door and waited like prey. I swore I could hear *everything*. The nightly wind howling outside, the distant crickets, the faint whisper of what might be a voice... Every creak in this vast building made my heart flutter. We had no clue what Krevall's plan was—only that he had one. As always, he was one step ahead.

I flinched at a footstep in the lobby, followed by many more. We had practiced how to walk silently during classes, yet Krevall used no stealth. He wanted us to hear him.

My pulse quickened at the short, scraping sound of a struck match.

Then came the storm.

There was no fire, but there were hundreds, perhaps thousands, of little brown beans rolling under the crack of our door.

Calabar. I frowned as a few of them slowed to a stop by my feet. While they were poisonous to consume or touch, they were harmless with our boots on.

My eyes widened when I noticed flames flickering at their edges. They weren't hot enough to set the floor on fire, but smoke curled upward, stinging my eyes. I whipped my head back and rubbed my face. There was a faint, greasy smell.

Krevall had soaked the beans in oil—turned them into kindling.

"It's in the air!" Boa shouted.

My lungs tightened, a cough itching to break free.

Silver dashed to the balcony door, rearing back his swords. A spine-chilling noise filled the room as the glass shattered against his blades, joining the hot beans on the floor.

A gust of wind blew through the opening where the door used to be.

We only coughed harder. Even with the balcony door gone, the air was unbearably thick. The wind was blowing in *our* direction, keeping the toxins trapped in. To escape the fumes, we needed to open the main door, which Krevall stood behind, or step onto the balcony. His plan relied on us choosing the latter so Nash could take his shot.

That left the main door.

A few shards of glass had pierced Silver's white sleeves. He winced and plucked out the pieces.

I darted past him and joined Cal by the door. She didn't stop me from unlocking it.

As soon as I heard the *click*, I stumbled back to keep my distance from Krevall. The dizziness from holding my breath made me gasp, filling my lungs with more toxic air. I folded over into a fit of coughs. My vision blurred, and when I finally looked up, Krevall's silhouette filled the doorway. He had wrapped a scarf around his nose and mouth to help protect him from the air, but his eyes were red like ours.

I forced myself to stand tall, gripping my dagger tightly, expecting him to rush into an attack.

But Krevall stood still. Perhaps our choice to invite him inside confused him—and in that moment of surprise, Cal flicked her wrist, spinning her dart in his direction.

Krevall's eyes narrowed as he raised his swords. Cal's dart bounced off and clattered on the floor.

She didn't hesitate before shooting another. And a third. He shielded his head and chest from the attacks, but she finally landed a dart to his calf.

Krevall yelled out, but he didn't drop his swords.

Before I knew it, I could barely breathe, and the fumes dragged me to the floor. The hot beans burned my palms as I pushed myself up, my vision swaying. Through the haze, Krevall drew his swords and stopped playing defense, just as I'd feared. With a quick swing, he slashed Cal's arm.

She staggered back, gripping the shallow wound. And in a fraction of a second, she fell.

I choked on the poisoned air. "Cal!"

"She has calabar in her bloodstream now," Krevall announced, his voice muffled by his scarf.

I looked over at Boa and Silver. They coughed hysterically as Cal flailed on the ground. They couldn't fight back—but unlike them, I cared for Cal enough to push through the pain. I gritted my teeth and took a single step toward Krevall.

He pressed his long blade down against Cal's neck. "Move again, and I'll kill her."

Stay calm, I ordered myself. *We have belladonna vials in the restroom. I just need to handle Krevall first.*

"Starfall..." The humor in his voice made me sick. "You and I both know that Cal would die anyway. She's the most expendable."

"Oh, shut it!"

He raised his brows and added pressure to the blade against her neck.

"I'll make it *your* choice, because I respect your game. You're a bold player."

I glued my lips shut.

"You can either stand here and watch Avarium die with me—*or* you can step onto the balcony and let Nash take his shot."

My hands shook. Cal wasn't moving anymore.

"I know you have belladonna somewhere in this room," Krevall continued. "If you step out, your boys and I can use it to save her. We need to have five winners, after all."

"Evaris," Silver choked out between coughs, "don't do anything stupid."

I tuned him out. He didn't know Cal like I did. He didn't understand the real reason why she worked so hard. He didn't even know her name was Calamity.

I sprinted to the balcony.

"Evaris!" Boa's voice cracked. "Stop!"

They had no time to get in my way. I practically dove over the shattered glass and onto the balcony. The railing was thick, and I ducked against it, hiding myself under Nash's range.

Krevall remained by Cal with a blade to her neck. The fabric around his mouth had slipped, revealing a twisted smile.

"You'll have to kill me yourself!" I yelled.

Boa aimed an arrow at Krevall, and Silver lifted his swords higher. They had every intention of killing him before he could get to me. But if they acted too soon, Krevall might slit Cal's throat and end her life for good.

"Drop your tools," I ordered them.

They looked over at me, their eyes sharp.

"Drop them!" I repeated, urging them to trust me. We could still follow Nash's plan, and they knew it.

Silver gulped and dropped his swords first. He muttered something to Boa that made him set his bow down too. Krevall squinted at them until they kicked their primary tools farther away. Only then did he leave Cal behind to approach me.

"You really want a sword over an arrow, Starfall?"

"Don't be a coward." My lips trembled. "If you want me dead, do it yourself."

Krevall stepped out and joined me on the balcony. "I'd hate to lose you."

I glared up at him, and he finally dropped his fake grin. He raised his sword in the moonlight, Cal's blood still marking the blade.

I clenched my eyes shut and raised my dagger in a helpless block, bracing for the worst-case scenario. My heart pounded out of my chest.

And just then, an arrow zipped through the air.

I opened my eyes at the sound of a falling body. Nash's arrow had struck Krevall's cheek, piercing all the way through his skull. He howled the most horrific noise into the wind as he melted right in front of me.

Without thinking, I raised my dagger and brought it down into Krevall's chest, eager to stop his struggling. It didn't work. I nearly struck him again, but Silver did it for me, sliding a single sword against his neck.

At last, our opponent stilled, but Silver stabbed him a second time anyway —as did I. Something in us didn't stop when Krevall did. We fought as though our lives depended on it, and at some point, Boa joined in, using one of Krevall's own blades against him.

When the three of us stopped to catch our breath, we rose to our feet and stared down at Krevall's mutilated body. I couldn't help but think of Avarium, back in Sitra, and how she had swung that log against Chima over and over. It didn't sound so crazy anymore. Even Silver didn't gag at the sight of blood tonight.

I gasped when I remembered Avarium on the floor, which seemed to snap Boa and Silver out of their dazes too. We rushed back inside, tracking blood into the room.

"Come on, please." I knelt beside Cal and shook her shoulder. "Wake up, please."

Silver pushed the dresser aside to unblock the restroom door. A moment later, he returned with a vial of belladonna we'd stored, along with a syringe. Boa poured the serum into the device and stabbed its needle into her thigh, right through her pants.

"Cal, come back to us..." I whispered.

Boa pushed the plunger down, injecting the serum.

We waited, hoping we weren't too late.

I squeezed her arm. "We need five winners. *Five.*"

With a gasp, Cal shot up into a seated position and looked around frantically.

"Hey." Silver leaned over, leveling with her. "It's okay. It's done."

She trembled as she continued scanning the room. Her eyes stopped on the balcony, and after a moment of processing what she was looking at, she sighed in relief, her shoulders dropping.

Boa yanked the syringe out of her leg when she wasn't looking.

Cal winced.

"Sorry!" he exclaimed.

She recovered quickly and smiled at him.

For a moment, everything was quiet.

CHAPTER 15

POST-MORTEM

Day 88 | 5 trainees remaining

♫ TOO FAR · WALLNERS ♫

Cal Avarium handed me a shovel. There were five in the storage shed—the perfect number this time.

We buried the body on the opposite side of the field from Gup. Nash choked up as Boa and Silver lowered his old friend into the grave we dug. His arms shook as he tried to scoop a pile of dirt on top.

"Don't worry." I placed a hand on his shoulder and guided him a few steps away. "We'll handle it."

He stood to the side, wiping tears as we covered what used to be Krevall with rocks, twigs, beetles, dead leaves...

When we were done, I pulled my notebook out and marked an *O* for fooling Krevall into getting shot. I marked an *X* for insisting that we bury him, and not burn him. Debts logged, duties paid.

We placed living flowers on one grave and dead ones on the other.

The guardians returned at sunrise after a week away. They found us sleepless on the grassy field, staring at the gray clouds above. It felt safer out here than within the haunting building where we had lost two of our own.

Commander Roz sighed at the blood stains and dirt on our clothes.

Professor Embre grinned; Doctor Blimmery turned away.

None of them said a word.

They spent a few minutes investigating our new grave before sending cleaners to the room where it happened.

About an hour later, the guardians ordered us to the dining hall for breakfast. Only one table remained where there used to be ten. It seated five instead of four—one chair for each of us. They didn't want us divided anymore. We had not misread their intentions after all.

Nash fell behind as the rest of us got seated. Cal was the first to look back at him.

My eyes watered when she called him over.

"Thank you," I said as Nash took the last chair.

He grinned back at me, and Silver patted him playfully on the shoulder. Boa laughed along as if he hadn't doubted Nash for a second.

A band of musicians arrived and set up their instruments in the corner, where they played a celebratory tune.

Professor Embre entered right after with a rolling cart of plates. "Congratulations on securing your spots as Academy graduates in the Force. Normally we don't have a final five this soon."

"So, what's next?" Boa's voice was hoarse.

Professor Embre reached our table and passed out breakfast. "We'll continue with the second half of our curriculum. This includes assignments to shadow real guardians at work. You'll each spend one day a month with a unit to learn the ropes." She tapped my shoulder. "Evaris, you'll go first. You're to meet your shadow unit leader in the common room at 6:00 tomorrow morning."

"Yes, Professor." The idea brought a smile to my face. Finally, I could leave this wretched building, even if just once a month. No more sabotage, no more filtrations, no more stress...

Professor Embre set the last plate and glass in front of me and left the dining hall.

Breakfast was chocolate cake and red juice. The guardians had never fed us junk before.

Without speaking, we took a few sugary bites and listened to the band's jumpy music. I thought of our first day at the Academy, when Cal had sat alone in this very dining hall. She hadn't cared what we thought of her. By protecting her brother, she had done something good. That was all that mattered.

I felt for the notepad in my pocket, and with the sweet taste of chocolate on my tongue, I promised I would never hold back from doing the right thing. Even if it impacted how people saw me, or put me in danger, or required me to log another *O* in this notepad—just as I'd done last night.

Silver's cough broke our silence. He raised his glass. "To the final five."

"To the final five," we echoed, taking our first sips.

We lowered our glasses in unison and shared a good laugh.

It was cranberry juice today.

Get Lost. in bonus content for
Avarium

Explore deleted scenes, author interviews, artwork, and more

LOSTISLANDPRESS.COM

ACKNOWLEDGMENTS

Let's roll the credits!

Thank you to Sebastian Delgado, my best friend and now-husband, for supporting me (and this book) like no other. I'm beyond excited to collaborate with you on another film project this year.

Joy Kabigting, I remember our time together as roommates fondly (don't worry, you weren't a creepy one). Not to be cringe, but I cherish you, dude.

Non Wannapa Lisa and Ploy Lungkham, I miss you always. Looking forward to seeing you in person again soon!

Thank you to Mom, Dad, and John for encouraging my love of books from a young age.

Natasha Orsh, for the gorgeous cover illustration.

Katie Flanagan, for editing this novella and helping me review our latest writing contest submissions at Lost Island Press.

My beta readers, for providing constructive criticism on an early draft of *Avarium*. You have no idea how much your feedback helped me:

S. J. Robert, Director Guppy Byleth, Kevin Konzen, Arpita Ghosh, Audrey Thackeray, Selena Ann, Hessa S, Veda Raman, Germaine Han, Concha Alvarez, Luke Veldkamp, Moxie F., M. L. Crowley, Hannah Wernecke, Tamara/Bookshelfenigma, Sabrey Moiraine, Olivia Chang, Dhru J, Victoria Nunweiller, Maria Wood, Avelia A. Shindyapin, Naba Khadija T, Amaryssa P, Mallory E., Grantaeus Gardner, S. E. Scott, Víctor Cantelar Sagrado

As always, sending my love to Grandpa Pete. *I will write another, and another, and another...*

Last but not least, thank *you* (yes, you) for spending some time with this story of mine.

If you're caught up with the main *Belladonna* series, I'm thrilled to share that I'm diving back into *Poisonous Remedy (Belladonna #3)* as we speak. It's an epic series finale that will cost me many tears to write.

I cannot, cannot, cannot wait!

ABOUT THE AUTHOR

MEL TORREFRANCA is a full-time author and founder of Lost Island Press. Her books feature morally gray characters, bold endings, and a pinch of awkward humor. Mel discovered her passion for writing at the age of seven and published her debut novel, *Leaving Wishville*, during high school. She also drinks way too many lattes.

MELTORREFRANCA.COM

ABOUT THE PUBLISHER

LOST ISLAND PRESS publishes dystopian, sci-fi, and fantasy books. Unlike mainstream presses, we don't publish everything for everyone. We publish for *you*. Our catalog offers grounded, character-driven stories that linger long after the last page. The kind you get lost in, that keep you up at night. And because our books have the same vibe, if you enjoy one, you'll enjoy them all.

LOSTISLANDPRESS.COM

Join our newsletter to claim a free ebook